Not THE BODYGUARD'S Boss

Other Books By Lorin Grace

American Homespun Series

Waking Lucy

Remembering Anna

Reforming Elizabeth

Healing Sarah

Artists & Billionaires

Mending Fences

Mending Christmas

Mending Walls

Mending Images

Mending Words

Mending Hearts

Hastings Security

Not the Bodyguard's Baby

Not the Bodyguard's Widow

Not the Bodyguard's Princess

Not the Bodyguard's Bride

Misadventures in Love

Miss Guided

Miss Oriented

Not THE BODYGUARD'S Boss

LORIN GRACE

Cover Design © 2019 Evan Frederickson and LJP Creative Graphics
Photos © iStock

Formatting by LJP Creative
Edits by Eschler Editing

Published by Currant Creek Press
North Logan, Utah

First edition: April 2020
ISBN: 978-1-970148-06-0

to Vlad

THE FIRST IMPALA

STANDING ON THE CURB, DEIDRE tapped the door of the SUV twice, signaling the driver he was safe to take the last of the VIPs away from the conference center. The glittering lobby was oddly silent after the three-hour society brunch for yet another charity. Deidre resisted the urge to stretch her shoulders. The unexpected overtime had put her at sixty-one hours for the week. She avoided the catering staff, circling the event-center ballroom, and entered the hallway to the ten-by-ten-foot room that served as the Hastings Security command post for the event. She stopped before entering to assess the situation when she heard raised voices coming from the room.

"Seriously? That's messed up. Abbie flattened one of your men last year at this event. Would you like to see the video?" The voice sounded like Mr. Alan's but might be one of the brothers'.

"Your sister is the exception."

"Hastings Security has seven stellar female bodyguards on staff, and we wish we could get more. And I'd match them against any man, any day." The voice must be Mr. Alan's as he hadn't counted Elle, the newest trainee graduate.

"We have had several female guards, but they keep washing out. More sick days, higher turnover. If they break a nail, they don't show up, and they leave their phones off." The speaker's derogatory tone begged to have her correct his opinions.

"We don't have that problem at Hastings Security. Take Deidre—she worked this morning's brunch. She's one of the best bodyguards we have, of any gender."

Deidre stepped closer to the door, the adage about eavesdroppers hearing no good coming to mind.

"The tall Latino?"

"Part Polynesian." Mr. Alan corrected the assumption, the same one he had made over three years ago when she'd joined Hastings.

"I saw her in the room, but the annual charity brunch is hardly a difficult venue," the voice sneered.

Enough. Deidre stepped into the doorway. "Any venue can become hazardous at any time." The man half turned in her direction, but Deidre kept her focus on Mr. Alan. "Here's my comms link. See you Monday." She left the room without acknowledging the other man.

"See? She isn't even working a full day."

Deidre didn't need to hear Alan's response. She was already well into overtime for the week and was only filling in for Alex Hastings, who'd picked up an unexpected new client. As for the chauvinist in the command center, Deidre could tell him exactly why he didn't know any decent female bodyguards. The problem stared him in the mirror every morning as he shaved his stubborn jawline.

In her car, Deidre flipped through her text messages. Her roommate had sent six, all begging her to **CALL NOW!!!!**

The call connected over the car's hands-free system. "Hey, Fiona, what's up?"

"You know the musical I was going to with my coworker?"

"You mean the double date I've been hearing about for two months since your friend won those tickets? Nope, never heard of it."

"Dee …" Fiona carried out the *e* into two syllables.

"Yes, I know you have tickets, the show is amazing, it's on opening night, and the guys are wearing tuxes."

"Well, she is sick. The whole 102-degree-fever-coughing-up-a-lung sick."

"Oh, yuck." Deidre pulled out into the heavy Saturday midday traffic typical for Chicago. In this part of town, it was mostly families running to soccer games or out to lunch.

"Please take her ticket. You have the perfect dress, and the guy she was going with is six five, so you can wear heels."

"You know my policy on blind dates."

"Have I told you about the show's reviews?"

"Only a gazillion times." The reviews were almost enough to cause Deidre to abandon caution and go.

"Amazing show! The songs will stay with you. Will join *Les Mis* as one of the greatest musicals ..."

Deidre turned into the garage of her apartment building. "Garage—I will lose you." She disconnected the call and spent the next three minutes coming up with excuses as she took the stairs to her fifth-floor condo.

Fiona met her at the door. "Please? I don't want to go with two guys. That would just be weird."

"I'm not going to an opening-night, black-tie event with someone else's boyfriend."

"He isn't her boyfriend."

"You're telling me a guy who's getting a tux for this isn't her boyfriend?"

"No, her boyfriend broke up with her last week. Liam is a friend of hers who owns a tux."

"So this is a fill-in date with a fill-in date?" Deidre took off her blazer and hung it in the closet. "This sounds a lot like a blind date, and I don't do blind dates."

"Honest, it's not. It would be a shame to let the ticket go to waste. You could wear the royal-blue dress or even one of the black ones."

Getting to wear the designer dress made the outing even more tempting. Abbie Hastings Harmon, wife of one of Chicago's wealthiest men, had given her the dress for her birthday last month. Deidre had protested a little, but Abbie had threatened to give her more dresses, claiming she'd never be the same size after the triplets came. "So if I go, just who is my date?"

"Liam is an old friend of Corrie's. He recently retired from the military. She thought the musical would be a fun way to get him back into real life."

Deidre had seen several opening-night shows, but most included keeping a close eye on her clients and missing half the show, scanning for threats. "Fine, I'll go. But so help me, Fiona, if this turns out to be a setup ..."

Fiona held up a hand. "I know you'll kill me four different ways and sink my body to the bottom of Lake Michigan."

"I'm glad we're clear on that." Deidre headed for the shower.

Liam groaned and tugged at the end of his crooked bow tie, regretting his impulsive decision to accept his friend's invitation to the opening night of the newest musical. Attending with his lifelong friend Corrie would have been uncomplicated, but now she was sick and he was going on what amounted to a blind date with a friend of a friend, of a friend.

The fifth time proved to be the charm, and the bow tie cooperated. Liam hurried to the car, not wanting to be late to the restaurant where they'd agreed to meet, as finding three people he'd never met before at the theater lobby would be nearly impossible. All he had was a description of Corrie's friend Fiona, which was vague enough to fit any number of blondes of average height.

Liam arrived at the restaurant three minutes late. So much for first impressions. The maître d' showed Liam to the table.

A cute blonde in a pink dress smiled at him. "Liam?" At his nod, she pointed to the empty chair. "I'm Fiona, or Fi, for short. This is my friend Kevyn and my roommate, Deidre."

The dark-haired woman in the blue dress reminded him of the female bodyguard Alan Hastings had defended that morning. Deidre had the same deep-caramel skin and chocolate eyes. But the resemblance ended there. She sipped demurely from her water glass. The lean arms and shoulders exposed by the dress were not the same the bodyguard had hidden under that boxy jacket. This woman might share the island heritage, but like her dangling earrings, she hailed from a different mold. Fluid, graceful, and gorgeous. Small talk filled the gaps as they ordered. Fiona worked with his friend Corrie as an accountant. Kevyn worked at a marketing firm and carried the conversation with stories of clients wanting outrageous campaigns.

Deidre kept looking at him oddly, as if she knew him. "Where did you say you worked?"

"I didn't. I started working for my father's firm two months ago, after I retired from the army."

Fiona laughed. "You two are in the same line of work."

Deidre narrowed her eyes. "You don't know Alan Hastings, do you?"

"Yes, I do."

The women exchanged a look as Deidre dug through her bag. "What does your father do?"

"My father is Simon Dermot. He owns Dermot Security."

"I'd say it was a pleasure meeting you again, but our meeting this morning wasn't a pleasure." She handed him a business card.

Deidre Ross

Hastings Security

"And for the record, I'll make good on Alan's promise and take you or any of your guards on—anyplace, anytime." A challenge laced her tone. She was serious but not eager to make the time and place now.

Kevyn laughed nervously, then started another story.

The steak in front of Liam lost its allure. He wondered how much of his conversation she'd overheard. Explaining that he'd been ranting because one of the bodyguards he'd scheduled hadn't shown wouldn't excuse his actions. Worse, the missing bodyguard was in the hospital after a car wreck. Not her fault.

Liam talked in a low voice, attempting to keep the conversation as private as possible. "I don't know how much you heard me tell Alan. I apologize if I offended you in any way. I was frustrated with one of our employees."

"Mia? How is she doing? I heard about her accident."

Liam tried to hide his surprise. "She broke her arm and has a concussion. How do you know Mia was hit by a car?"

"As you pointed out this morning, there are not many female bodyguards in Chicago." Deidre rolled her eyes and followed his lead, leaning in close. "The offer stands, but let's spar some other time. Fiona has been looking forward to this musical for weeks. I don't think she would appreciate me pinning you to the floor tonight. Besides, I might break a nail."

Fiona and Kevyn studied their plates. What a disaster. If only Deidre hadn't walked in on him in the middle of a frustrating morning. The news of the accident had come moments after his rant. To be fair, he would have ranted over any missing employee, although perhaps not for so long. Earlier that week, he'd let another female guard go and, in frustration, made unfair generalizations.

Everyone at the table pretended to enjoy the rest of the dinner. Only Fiona ordered dessert.

Every positive review Fiona had mentioned was spot on. The soundtrack would be on Deidre's phone before she went to bed. The only thing that would make the musical more enjoyable was if she didn't have to deal with the man sitting next to her. Why did all the handsome ones have fatal flaws? She should have excused herself the moment she recognized Liam. Pled a headache or cramps. But Fiona would murder her for leaving, and the musical was worth enduring his presence.

She didn't fool herself with the lie that she would never see him again. There would be future events they both worked. Simon Dermot's firm oversaw Preston Harmon's security, which included his wife, the former Abbie Hastings, a legend among bodyguards, both female and male. Deidre visited Abbie only occasionally as a friend, but chances were she would run into Liam again.

Abbie's marriage had left a huge hole at Hastings Security, one Deidre and her coworkers had been struggling to fill. Not that anyone was asking them to work harder. From the day Hastings hired her, they'd treated Deidre as an equal. Deidre suspected the open-mindedness displayed by Jethro Hastings had a lot to do with his wife, who was still involved in the industry. Unlike Deidre's years with the police force, not once had any coworker at Hastings cited her gender as a liability. In fact, they considered it an asset as valuable as her years of martial-arts training. Her promotions and pay reflected that. Too bad Liam couldn't appreciate her skills.

A couple, most likely the doomed lovers, danced across the stage singing a tune far happier than Deidre's mood. Fiona clapped loudly as the song ended. Fortunately, Deidre hadn't ruined her roommate's night. If only she'd kept her mouth shut and not blurted out what she'd been thinking all day. There had to be several thousand single men in the greater Chicago area. What were the chances? Should she schedule a Lyft or Uber to get home? Fiona and Kevyn had two passes to an after party. There would be time to worry about that later. Deidre forced herself to focus on the stage and pretended she didn't notice the understated spiciness of the bodyguard's cologne. She would not allow Liam's presence to steal all the joy of the evening.

NEW-CLIENT MEETING, TUESDAY 9:00 A.M. Mr. Hastings and Mr. Alan request your presence.

The office manager always used *mister* before the first names of the four Hastings brothers so as not to confuse them with their father, Jethro.

Deidre reread the message. She'd never been to a new-client meeting before. Even though she'd taken the lead on some small jobs, Jethro and Mr. Adam always assigned her the job after signing the client. Currently, she led the security detail for musician September Platt. Not that there was much to do now that September was back from her mini music tour and resting with her infant daughter, content to stay out of the public eye. Which was why, today, Deidre was heading up what should have been Mr. Alex's detail. She texted back the only answer she could. **I'll be there. Anything I need to prep?**

The receptionist answered. **No, Mr. Alan will make sure we cover your shift until the meeting is over.**

Thanks.

If she'd had more time to ponder the situation, she would have; however, her current client had received another series of stalker emails last week, yet couldn't cancel her appearance at a children's cancer unit today. And the client deserved Deidre's full attention.

Fortunately, with the layers of security at the children's hospital, the event had been undisturbed, unlike Deidre's thoughts. A new-client meeting could mean a promotion to detail coordinator. With the oldest Hastings brother, Adam, traveling more and more, a position would soon open.

A female detail coordinator—take that, Mr. Liam women-don't-make-good-bodyguards Dermot. No, she hadn't been obsessing about him the last two days, wishing she'd said something witty or that he wasn't the perfect height or less handsome. Fiona hadn't stopped talking about his looks, trying to get Deidre to see Liam in a different light, insisting he was one of the good guys.

But Deidre had put up with enough of his kind working with the police department. Gender and ability were not mutually exclusive attributes. Some men, and even some women, couldn't see that. Graduate at the top of your class from the academy? Fluke. Take part in the world taekwondo championships? Yes, but you didn't medal. It didn't matter what the accomplishment was—some people simply refused to see beyond gender.

A little girl tugged on her pant leg. "Are you a strong guy like him?" The child pointed across the room to another security guard.

Deidre crouched down to be on the girl's level. "Yes, I am."

"I am too. See my cape?" The girl turned to show off the red cape flowing down her back. "I will be a superhero when I grow up. Joey says that's dumb, that girls grow up to be princesses. But I don't want to be a princess. They aren't strong."

"I think princesses can be very strong—like Cinderella, she worked hard and still was happy, even though she had a hard life. And Beauty was very brave to change places with her father and live with a beast. Just because someone has huge muscles doesn't mean they are strong inside." At least the versions of the fairy tales the little girl would have heard went that way.

The little girl furrowed her brow. "So they are like you, strong and pretty?"

"No, some are stronger, like you."

The girl nodded and moved off. Deidre stood and scanned the room, her gaze drawn back to the little girl in the red cape. Probably three years old—about the same age one little girl would have been. Would she have been as inquisitive?

A voice came over her earpiece. "Two minutes."

Deidre moved to the doorway of the playroom and checked the hallway. She nodded to a guard near the elevator, then waited. If anyone asked what most of her job comprised, she would tell them waiting, and mostly waiting for nothing to happen. Now she only had to wait for tomorrow.

"This is a mistake." Liam sat in the leather chair on the other side of the desk, across from his father.

The Dermot Security logo flashed across the screen before Simon's computer went black. "No, it isn't. We have little choice in the matter. As you pointed out, we don't have another female with the skill set required for this job. Mrs. Harmon's tough on her bodyguards. The last thing we want is for her to not have faith in them while she's in labor and delivery. You should have seen her in action last year. I haven't seen a cooler head as she worked to defuse the bomb."

"Fake bomb."

"We didn't know that at the time. Have you seen the video of her taking out Patrick Vonn?"

Liam crossed his arms. "You have only shown it to me a half dozen times. Very nice parlor trick." Fancy moves had their place but were nearly useless in real-life situations.

"It's more than a trick to take down an experienced bodyguard with seventy pounds on you."

"I will concede Mrs. Harmon was an excellent bodyguard, but she isn't a Hastings bodyguard anymore."

Simon gathered his phone and some papers. "True, but she will always think like a bodyguard. She was with the Secret Service for a time. Having one of the female guards she helped train on your detail during the last few weeks of her pregnancy and during the delivery will go a long way toward keeping her happy. It's unfortunate the three we've hired in the past few months haven't worked out. Well, Mia will, after she heals from the car accident."

"I ranted about her missing the charity brunch to Alan Hastings. Had I known she was on her way to the ER after the driver ran the stoplight, I wouldn't have complained about female bodyguards."

"You what?"

"You heard me. I shot off my mouth when I shouldn't have. Considering one of their female guards heard me and ended up being my disaster of a blind date that night, I thought you should know." He hoped she wouldn't be the one chosen for the job—although last night's internet search confirmed Ms. Deidre Ross would probably be Mrs. Harmon's number-one pick.

"The military should have taught you to control your mouth. Do you know how much almost any security firm would pay to have one of Hastings's trained bodyguards on their detail? Especially one trained by Abbie and her mother? The woman who is the 'nanny' for the Crawfords could incapacitate a man while singing the child to sleep and the kid wouldn't know anything happened. And at our Security Team Olympics last year, one of the Hastings women took out half our martial-arts group in the first round. I hear she took over training after Jethro forced Abbie to stop once he discovered he had three grandbabies on the way."

"You are exaggerating."

"I wish I were. Every woman who wants into the industry goes to Hastings first. We were lucky we got Mia. Abbie liked her too."

Liam held up his hands. "Fine, I get it. Hastings is not only our biggest competitor, they are the best."

"Which is why we are fortunate to be on the same team and have an alliance. We watch each other's backs. The only time we compete is at the security Olympics. I haven't competed with Jethro over clients for years, and you know we both refer to each other when we can."

"You are sure contracting one of Hastings's guards is the only way?"

"Without Mia, yes. Jethro wants Abbie to be comfortable more than we do. Don't worry. He'll loan us his best."

Liam wasn't worried about getting the best. He was worried the best would be Deidre Ross.

"GO ON INTO MR. HASTINGS office. The client was early." The new receptionist pointed the way as if Deidre didn't know the office after three years.

Deidre checked her watch. She was ten minutes early. Just how early had the client been? The first person she saw as she opened the door was Alan, arms crossed, a scowl on his face. The second was Liam Dermot, a similar expression on his. Deidre pasted on her work smile so as to not add to the tension.

Jethro stood. "Deidre, come in. You didn't miss anything significant."

Taking one of the empty chairs, Deidre studied the men. She had missed something. Odd. Jethro rarely lied.

Alan turned to her. "Liam was apologizing to me for some remarks he made on Saturday."

"I believe I owe Miss Ross an apology too. I watched a video of the mini Olympics. I believe you are correct. You could take on most of our employees and win any day."

Most? For her boss's sake, she bit back the retort that came to mind. "I thought this was a client meeting?" She directed her remark to Jethro.

Jethro sat back down behind the desk. "It is, of a sort. Saturday morning, one of Dermot's guards was T-boned by a texting driver. They released her from the hospital yesterday, but she has a broken arm and a concussion. Unfortunately, she was a critical part of Abbie's security detail. Part of her assignment was to be in the delivery room and protect Abbie and the children, if necessary. You know Abbie well enough to understand she doesn't want just anyone in there. Dermot Security would like to contract you out for the next six weeks or more until their team member can return to work. The end of the assignment ultimately depends on when my grandsons make their entry into the world."

"Why me?" There was no way on earth she wanted to work with Liam, even for Abbie's sake.

"I spoke with Abbie last night, and she chose you," said Jethro. "She likes your style and felt you were not too close of friends that it could be a distraction. Her only concern was that you might have problems in the delivery room. She mentioned hospitals are not your favorite place."

Deidre nodded but refused to give anything away. "Hospitals aren't anyone's favorite place, are they? The delivery room won't be a problem." She would not be the one in labor.

Liam leaned forward. "Then, you are willing?"

"I'm not sure. What about my current clients?"

Alan tapped on his tablet. "I've moved a few things around. We will cover your schedule. The only issue is the training we scheduled you to do."

"We will work with you on flexible hours, other than any medical appointments Abbie has, and the delivery," said Liam.

"So I can train as long as Abbie's babies don't come that morning?"

"We can let everyone know that if you don't show, they are to do a normal conditioning routine." Alan made a note on his tablet.

"That works for us," said Liam.

Deidre looked to Jethro. "How do you feel about this arrangement? Is having me guard your daughter and your grandsons too much of a conflict?"

Jethro leaned on his desk. "Melanie and I discussed this last night. If they wanted one of our sons, I'd have to answer yes. But you have more of a professional friendship with Abbie, so I don't consider that a conflict. Dermot security has agreed to pay you time and a quarter, with another quarter to Hastings, knowing we will have to work to fill the rather large hole you'll leave for the next six weeks."

Did Dermot realize how much they would be paying her? Not that it mattered. She looked at Liam. The thin line of his lips told her he knew exactly what the fee for her services would be. Likely more than he made.

Liam tapped on his phone. "We will also pay you double for overtime active hours. You will be on call 24/7 and will reside on-site at the estate, as the delivery isn't something that can be scheduled."

Deidre took a certain amount of delight in Liam's begrudging offer. Obviously, there had already been quite a bit of negotiating before they'd presented her with the plan. "If Abbie is comfortable with me protecting her, I'll take it. When do I meet the rest of the detail?"

Liam extended his hand. "We are the detail. There will be more guards at the hospital, but they will come from Mr. Harmon's detail and even his parents'. That part is fluid."

Not what she expected. Could she back out? Not with Jethro smiling. Deidre shook Liam's hand and wished she'd negotiated for more. Like getting paid not to show him exactly how good a female bodyguard could be.

Liam stood near the doorway across the room known as the Yellow Parlor, despite its being decorated mostly in tans and browns. Deidre and Mrs. Abbie Harmon held a semiprivate conversation. Mrs. Harmon seemed more pleased about the bodyguard arrangement than Deidre.

He studied the woman he would spend most of the next six weeks with. She was only a few inches shorter than his six foot five, a rarity he'd noticed at the restaurant. He didn't doubt that she could take him down in a sparring match. Overconfidence was not an asset for a bodyguard. Neither was not being confident enough. The latter was the most dangerous. Deidre's posture exuded confidence, and her movements were more fluid and graceful than the men he was used to working with.

So far, he'd found Deidre to be levelheaded. Last Saturday, he half expected her to storm out of the restaurant like his ex-girlfriend, but Deidre had put her friend's welfare first. Although she had been distant after their exchange at the restaurant, she hadn't continued the argument or ignored him when he spoke. And she'd graciously accepted his offer for a ride home and listened to his apologies. Today, she hadn't balked when informed she would live at the Harmon mansion and be on call 24/7. Since accepting the job, he'd talked to her as little as possible. Her questions had been technical, and he'd answered her by giving her the electronic file containing various background checks and itineraries. Planning for any birth wasn't easy, but the Harmon triplets' birth was made more difficult since the projected due date, set at thirty-six weeks or later, could be as early as any minute. Dozens of plans covering NICU, infant mortality, and various lengths of hospital stays had been carefully drawn up. Mrs. Harmon's intent to have the babies naturally was only possible under certain conditions.

Instead of reading over the hundreds of pages of information during their drive, Deidre had looked out the window, the deafening silence on the drive from her office to the estate not boding well for their working relationship. If she hadn't been eavesdropping, there wouldn't be a problem. He'd apologized.

What more could he do?

Liam waited for the conversation across the room to end, though it looked like the women had only gotten started. Mr. Hastings had indicated they were not close friends. Perhaps he was wrong. Liam mentally reviewed the plans Deidre had ignored during their drive.

Inside the Harmon estate, there was little for either of them to do other than wait for Mrs. Harmon to go into labor, which no one wanted for at least another four weeks. The regular detail took care of the estate security. With Mrs. Harmon on partial bed rest and a nurse checking in on her every other day, there wasn't likely to be much activity for Liam and Deidre outside of doctor's appointments. This suited Liam fine as some procedures to protect a principal, such as pushing them to the ground, could harm Mrs. Harmon as much as the danger they were evading. A shopping trip could all too easily turn into a disaster.

Liam grew restless. Perhaps they were taking so long to see if he would react. He pulled out his phone and checked the calendar. "Familiarize Deidre with the hospital" was the only item left on the day's checklist. The chaos of a triplet birth would be the easiest point for the paparazzi or a kidnapper to gain access to the family. Knowing the floor plan and recognizing the hospital staff without checking tags was essential.

But because of various privacy laws, they couldn't vet the nurses and hospital staff like they would for other events. However, they could tour the maternity floor in the company of a hospital administrator and meet the staff that regularly worked there during one of the four shifts. Liam had met most of the staff last week, but Deidre needed to recognize them on sight too.

Liam eyed the chair next to the door. Technically, he wasn't on duty when inside the house. He could sit. Abbie, then Deidre, glanced his way. It was obvious they were talking about him. No, he would continue to stand. Sitting would show weakness, and Deidre couldn't see him as a weak boss, given the already low opinion she had of him. To pass the time, he counted to one hundred in all the languages he knew. When he became bored with that, he stopped at fifty-nine in Farsi and started reciting Shakespearean sonnets.

Abbie looked over Deidre's shoulder. "He is the stiffest bodyguard I've ever seen."

"Do you think he's competent?" Abbie's opinion mattered not only because she was the client, but because she was perhaps the best female bodyguard the city had ever seen.

"He has only been on my detail the last month and a half or so. Came to work for Simon right out of the military, and it shows. Simon thinks he's the right man for the job, and I've learned to trust him. The only real mistake Simon ever made was hiring Patrick Vonn. In Simon's defense, though, Patrick had a clean background. Only my brothers knew what a weasel he was."

Deidre laughed. The video of Abbie flipping Patrick on his backside was legendary in the security community. Every female bodyguard at Hastings had perfected Abbie's signature move. Patrick was now serving time in Massachusetts for his role in a fake bombing.

Deidre used a distorted reflection of Liam in the lamp nearest her to study her new boss, the curve of the lamp base giving him a potbelly. She doubted he would ever let that happen. "So you've seen Liam in action?"

"I watched him at the gym, and I've seen a video of his shooting. Poor Simon. I am so picky, he has to provide me with so much information. Simon didn't have any females last year, and he's been trying to recruit them. Two of his hires were women I had trained a couple years ago but didn't make the cut. Do you remember Julie?"

"The one who spent the entire shift flirting with Alex on the comms?"

"Yes, that's her. Simon hired her last month, and when she made the moves on Liam, he got rid of her faster than Alex did."

One point for Liam. Plus, if Julie had been one of the female bodyguards he'd worked with, he had a right to complain. "What about the woman I am replacing? Mia?"

"Mia was good. I would have liked to train her more to get her up to our level. She had the skills and instincts, but Simon made her a better offer, and she jumped at the opportunity to not be at entry level. I had confidence she'd work well for my delivery detail, as her observation skills are almost as good as yours. I hope she can recover from the car accident and come back to be part of my personal detail after the babies are here."

"I heard she has a broken arm." If the break heals correctly, Mia could return to work full time in two months and on light duty before that.

Abbie looked over Deidre's shoulder a second time. "I wish he would relax. It isn't like you will attack me. He doesn't need to be in here at all."

"I went to the theater with him on Saturday. I don't know if *relax* is in his vocabulary. I didn't realize it was possible to sit at attention in one of those upholstered chairs."

Abbie raised a brow at the admission. "I'm sure there is more to the story. You can share that with me when he isn't lurking about." She stretched her back and adjusted her position. "I know I had my dad ask you this already, but I need to know for myself. Can you handle being in a delivery room?"

The question was loaded and fair. "I believe I can. Liam and I are touring the hospital later. If anything triggers even the smallest doubt, I'll recommend someone else today. Tonie is more than ready for this kind of job."

Thought lines furrowed Abbie's brow. "I would rather you be the one at the hospital with me. I hope you've healed, but if there's something that makes it too painful for you to take this job … no hard feelings between us, okay? I don't want to cause you pain."

"Thanks." Deidre checked the reflection in the lamp again. "We should probably go to the hospital. If he stands like that much longer, he's liable to lose his mind."

"You're no fun. I wanted to see how long he could stand at attention."

Deidre rolled her eyes at Abbie and crossed the room. She nodded at Liam but didn't speak. There was no need. He led her out of the room.

THE HOSPITAL TOUR TOOK AN hour and twenty-seven minutes. Waiting for Deidre to explore the access and exit points took another fifty-three. Liam frowned. He had all the information she needed in the file he'd sent to her phone. Why waste time redoing his work?

Deidre stood at the door of the room Abbie would use after the babies were born. "The room on the opposite corner has better sight lines."

"As noted in the report I gave you, that room is too small to accommodate three bassinets and visitors." Liam didn't bother keeping the annoyance out of his voice.

"I am sure you wrote a comprehensive plan; however, in the three hours I've had on this assignment, I have not yet had time to review the document. Since the maternity ward is more than half empty, I thought this was the best time for me to see the layout and what I am working with. You hired me to protect Abbie. I will do things to her standards." She pivoted and paced off the distance to the stairwell.

Torn between annoyance and admiration, Liam kept his thoughts to himself. Alan had been right to defend her skills. She'd verified all of the information he had when he took the assignment. Her personality could be improved. Then again, off-putting was a benefit to a bodyguard, especially when it was confused with intimidating. He avoided talking to Deidre as she continued her inspection of the nursery area and the two large delivery rooms.

"Any chance we can have the one on the north?"

Liam took several seconds to realize she was referring to the room at his left. "If no one is here, yes. I've already put in a request. The problem is that the hospital can't predict how many women will be here, though they do save these rooms for multiple births or ones where complications are expected. The four surgical suites have the same issue. One is much larger and preferred, if needed."

"Then I think I've seen everything I need to. I'll let you know if I have questions after reading your report. I assume it has the full floor plan?"

Liam followed her to the elevator. "Color coded."

"Good." The empty elevator arrived. Deidre stepped in first and got the far corner spot. Liam took the other one, impressed that she had automatically taken the better position.

When the doors closed, she spoke quietly. "You don't want me here, do you?"

"It isn't my decision. Mrs. Harmon insists on having a female bodyguard in the room. We had to replace Mia, and Mrs. Harmon chose you."

"Getting T-boned by a texting driver running a red was not Mia's fault. And it wasn't mine. In fact, the driver was a male, so you can't even blame it on womankind. Can you please lose some of your attitude?"

He was texting his girlfriend. The elevator doors opened, admitting an elderly couple, and Liam bit back his retort.

"Would you mind dropping me off at the Hastings offices? My car is there, and I'll need more clothing than what's in my go-bag if I'm going to live on-site for the next few weeks."

This reasonable request hadn't been part of his plan. "I still need to get you your security credentials for the estate."

"You can do that while I'm moving my things. I can get them from you when I get back."

"You won't be able to get in the gate."

"I will if you put me on the visitor list for the day."

She was right. He pulled up in front of the Hastings Security offices. "What time should I tell them to expect you?"

Deidre checked her watch. "Around nineteen hundred."

"That's three hours!"

"Yes, I know. I need to take care of some things at Hastings first. See you later." She shut the car door behind her.

Liam drove to the Dermot Security offices. She'd ruined his schedule, which hadn't included her getting her personal items or returning to Hastings. Now he had to rearrange things to accommodate her. Just who was the boss here?

There wasn't much work for Deidre to do at the office—nothing she couldn't do from the Hastings Security app. But there was the gym, and there might be someone to spar with. If she didn't work out her annoyance, she might make good on her threat to take Liam down anytime, anywhere. Dermot Security had presumably hired her for her skills, yet whenever she used them, Liam got annoyed. When exactly was she supposed to have read his report and what type of guard would she be if she didn't verify what she could?

Silence greeted her in the gym. No music, no clanking of weights, and no whir of the treadmills. Four o'clock wasn't the most popular time, but usually there was someone working out before a night shift. Deidre changed in the locker room, then returned to the empty gym. Mortimer the sparring dummy would have to do. The music of her favorite workout playlist flowed through the Bluetooth speakers, chasing away the silence.

Mortimer's expression remained stoic as she pummeled him with kick after punch. He didn't move either, which made him not much of a challenge. The music changed, and Deidre worked through several martial-arts forms. Good thing she was alone. Her focus wasn't in her workout.

Kickboxing Mortimer was more satisfying. A series of ninja-worthy moves, useless for anything other than show or to beat up inanimate objects, finished her workout. Her last kick was met with clapping.

Alan sat on the weight bench. "I'm impressed."

"Don't be. Those moves are just for show. In real life, a flip kick would only give your opponent time to attack." Deidre used a towel to wipe her face.

"Still, I don't think I'd want to spar with you today. I'd lose for sure."

Deidre nodded at his tie. "You're not exactly dressed for a sparring match."

"No, I'm dressed to accompany my client to a speech, which is over, so I came down to change clothes. Do you want to spar?" Alan pulled off his tie.

A glance at the clock told Deidre she had already used almost an hour of her time. "I'd better not. I have to be back at your sister's estate in a couple hours, and I have to drop by my condo and get a few things."

"Dare I ask how things with Liam Dermot went?"

"I feel like I need to prove myself. I don't know how to prove to him just how skilled a female bodyguard can be, short of using him as a sparring dummy."

Alan chuckled. "I think he will figure it out soon. You're both living at Abbie's, right?"

"On call 24/7 until your nephews appear."

"I hope you are in for at least three boring weeks then. I want them "fully baked," as Abbie puts it." Alan's grin reached ear to ear.

"A little excited to be an uncle?"

"Maybe. I'm glad you're the one who'll be guarding Abbie. She won't let anyone but Mom in the room during the delivery. I thought she'd let Alex, but he's too busy with his client, or wife, or . . ." Alan's voice faded. No one could explain Alex's sudden marriage.

"I'm still confused by his situation."

Alan shrugged. "It's Alex. He'll get his job sorted out eventually. Good luck working with Liam. Despite what you heard the other morning, I don't think he's—"

"Chauvinistic? Opinionated? Controlling? All of the above?"

"My brothers had to chill out when they got out of the service. It took them a few months to dial down their intensity. Remember when Ben started with us? Now he regularly asks for women to be on his team."

Deidre hung her towel around her neck. "Didn't you serve too?"

"Didn't qualify. I have the rare privilege of being born with only one kidney, which is why I only get the light assignments. Speaking of which, I'd better get going." Alan dusted off his pants.

"Light assignments? I thought you had some big ones too."

"Maybe." He waved as he left.

Deidre turned off her music, plunging the gym into silence again.

Liam stopped at the open door to his father's office. The room was empty.

"Looking for me?" His father's voice came from behind him.

"Just wanted to say hi. I'm off to the estate, and I don't expect to be back for a few days."

"How is the Hastings guard going to work out?"

"She's skilled."

"Undoubtedly. Jethro Hastings wouldn't have her on his payroll if she wasn't. And he wouldn't have told me she's his best, either." Simon waved Liam into his office ahead of him.

"I think it may be a long six weeks. She doesn't have Mia's personality."

"Ms. Ross has been friendly every time I've interacted with her. You didn't offend her again, did you?"

"Again? No. And I apologized for what she overheard. I was upset at Mia—"

Simon laid a hand on Liam's shoulder. "You can be upset with one person without taking on the whole industry. Even if your morning was disrupted, Mia had the best/worst no-show excuse this year."

"I guess I'm not used to thinking about the fact that bad things happen State-side too. And after the women we fired…" Liam shrugged. His father had heard the lecture before.

"I believe Ms. Ross used to be with the Chicago PD. I bet your comments are not the first she's heard about her gender being incapable of doing the job."

If Liam had been twelve, the frown his father gave him would have had him begging for a second chance. "You've been telling me since I was fifteen that I'm too quick to judge. I really don't think all women are incapable of doing the job. It's just been my experience since getting home." He'd learned in the army that most women were as competent as the men, if not more so. But when a male had a problem, the incident was never blamed on gender. Even official military policy didn't blame a woman for being female when mistakes were made, as some of the men did. Had he? Maybe?

Simon's lecture wasn't over. "It will take more than a few words to convince Ms. Ross you believe she's competent. And you need to believe it. Not because I say so or because Jethro Hastings does. There's a chance someone will try to get into the delivery room to take photos. Any child of someone as wealthy as the Harmons is always in danger from some disgruntled or desperate person. The hospital already has a protocol in place for kidnapping. It's been proven to be a successful deterrent, but if there is a threat, you need to trust each other so you can respond without hesitation. And as the leader of your detail, it's your responsibility to build that trust and make sure she feels the same."

"But I can't control what she thinks of me."

"No, but you can make sure you don't give her a reason to doubt you trust her. Think about what you did to build trust with your fellow soldiers and apply what you know."

Liam pondered. "What would you suggest? I don't think a three-day survival hike will work in this situation."

"That's for you to figure out. Soon." Simon looked at his watch. "I have an appointment I can't miss. Anything else?"

"Thanks, Dad." Liam left the office no wiser than when he'd entered.

USUALLY, STAYING ON-SITE MEANT MIDCLASS hotel accommodations at best. The employee suite that would be Deidre's home for the next few weeks felt like a home, the bed comfortable enough to have kept her from waking at her normal 5:00 a.m. Her only regret about the extra hour of sleep was what Liam would think of her.

Unsurprisingly, the Harmon's home gym was amazing. Deidre made a mental note to grab her swimsuit next time she was back at the condo to try the swim spa, the water equivalent of a treadmill. The sparring dummy didn't have a broken nose. Otherwise, he could have been Mortimer's less beat-up twin. After walking around the room twice, Deidre ran a few miles on the treadmill. She plugged her phone into the speakers and brought up her playlist, keeping the volume loud enough to motivate her but not enough to be heard beyond the room.

She had just completed her third mile when a reflection in the mirror caused her to misstep. She caught herself and continued running. Liam's presence would not change her workout. Not even her music, unless he asked. She pretended not to notice him adjust the weight machine. He set it to a reasonable training weight. Good, he wasn't stupid enough to injure himself trying to impress her. Unfortunately, some of the thoughts running through Deidre's mind were not as bright—she hadn't planned on sparring with the dummy after last night's workout, but maybe a little exhibition wouldn't hurt. But he hadn't looked at her in the mirror. Chances were he wouldn't be impressed with the showy moves anyway.

After completing her ten miles, Deidre moved to the mat, where the angle of the mirrors didn't reflect Liam's every move. It wasn't just him. Like any other woman, she could admire a well-toned body. The fact she admired Liam's was merely an unfortunate coincidence.

Narrowing her focus until only the space around her existed, she moved through the forms of several martial-arts variations, then finished and bowed to her invisible instructor before moving into some classic stretches.

Liam joined her on the floor. "Do you always work out in the morning?"

"When I can. Is it wise for us to both be in here?"

"I don't see a problem with it."

"I mean since we are both on call. If we're both in workout clothes, there could be a problem."

"With the nurse monitoring Mrs. Harmon, we should have ample warning."

"Complications with a pregnancy can happen faster than you think." Deidre showed off with a set of splits.

"I see your point. Would you prefer to schedule workouts or just coordinate so we can avoid the overlap?"

"That depends on how you want to do the rotation schedules. I've been contemplating an eight-hour sleep schedule. It will wreak havoc on my night and day, but there's a better chance of being rested when the babies make their debut."

"How would that work?"

"Awake eight, sleep eight, repeat. So sometimes I sleep in the day, other times in the evening or at night. What I don't know is if such a schedule will make me less alert. My other option is to try for a full ten hours every night."

"I hadn't thought of modifying sleep patterns. You could try the eight-hour rotation for the next few days. If you are awake for Mrs. Harmon's doctor appointment Friday, on Saturday, I can give you a simple test and you'll know if the pattern works."

Deidre opened her mouth to retort, then realized he'd agreed with her. "Then I'll try it."

"If I think your experiment may be adversely affecting you, will you trust my judgment?"

"I don't know. We haven't even known each other a week. How would you know if I was any different from normal?"

"Good point. I did just watch you focus on your forms. I could use that as a measure." Liam completed his hamstring stretch, then stood, offering her a hand up. Deidre took it. His grip was firm, friendly. He was offering more than help off the mat, yet he didn't hold her hand longer than needed before stepping back. "Have you had breakfast?"

"No." Where was he going with this? As eating before a heavy workout wasn't the wisest idea, he had to know she wouldn't have eaten before coming to the gym.

"Meet you in the kitchen in twenty?" As she walked to the exit, Liam beside her, she realized that unlike a gym, where she could escape into the locker room, they would both have to traverse the length of the house to the rooms assigned them.

"Why?"

"So we can go over the schedule for the next few days. I don't want to accidentally wake you up."

He was trying too hard but not in a date-me-I'm-what-you-need type way. Maybe he, too, realized what a disaster yesterday was. "Fine. I'll see you in twenty." She entered her suite.

If he was willing to try, she could too.

Liam rushed through his shower to beat Deidre to the employee kitchen. He hadn't expected her to agree to eat with him. She was right. They didn't know each other. Had they only met in the Hastings office yesterday morning, the animosity between them wouldn't exist.

He arrived to find Deidre already sitting at one of the tables in the large kitchen dining area, having served herself a plate of eggs and an orange. A few of her natural curls hung damp around her face, the rest of her hair up in a bun. She gave him a half smile and saluted him with her fork. She shouldn't have been able to beat him. Even if he had taken the time to shave. Liam dished himself a plate of eggs, adding tomatoes, peppers, and avocado, then sat across the table from her.

She waited until he sat down before speaking. "I finished reading your report last night. It was very thorough. There is only one wild card you didn't account for."

Liam chewed slowly so he didn't have to answer. What could he have missed? He couldn't think of anything. Mrs. Harmon had even insisted on seeing the plan. "What?"

"Someone using a laboring woman to get access to the floor."

"How could they arrange that?"

"It would take a bit of planning, tracking several women who are expecting. Perhaps using one of the free clinics to find her, then waiting until Abbie goes into labor. Find the next woman due and jump-start the contractions using the same drugs the hospital doctors do. Then drive her across town to the emergency room. The emergency room examines her and sends her up to the floor."

"Do you think someone would do that?"

Deidre finished her eggs and pushed the plate aside. "There are over 180 babies born in Cook County each day. It wouldn't be too hard to find a dozen mothers who would agree to the scheme for a few thousand dollars and the opportunity to give birth in one of the nicer hospitals."

Liam toyed with his eggs. Possible? Yes. Probable? He didn't have an answer for that. "Do you think it's likely?"

"Depends on how desperate the paparazzi are. A birth gives a supposed new father or grandparent unquestioned access to the floor. No one will look at them too closely. The hospital staff is more concerned for the birth, as they should be."

"So what do we look for?" Liam opened his phone and took notes. Her idea had merit, and they needed a plan to deal with it.

"Not sure. Most of the new and birthing moms will be existing patients of a doctor with hospital privileges. We would look for an unexpected patient, but with privacy laws, I don't know if we can be told that. Or if we watch all prospective fathers and grandparents with equal suspicion."

Liam made a note in his phone. "I'll ask the hospital administrator if they can alert us to any patients who are emergency-room admissions. They are anxious that there not be an incident like the King Edward VII's Hospital in 2012."

Deidre studied the ceiling for a moment. "Was that when the Australian radio hosts called and tricked the nurse into divulging information about the duchess?"

"Yes, the nurse later committed suicide. As invasion of privacy goes, the information divulged by the poor nurse was mild. The radio hosts were playing a prank; they didn't think they would get any information. They later apologized. Mrs. Harmon's hospital doesn't want a single word or photo out there that hasn't come through official channels, which is why they have been so good about working with us as much as the law allows."

"A home birth would be so much simpler." Deidre took a cranberry muffin from the basket in the center of the table.

"Unfortunately, triplets prevent that. I would let the Harmons know they should have planned this better and tried for singletons, but I don't think they'd appreciate the suggestion." He watched as she took a large bite. "Those are full of white flour and sugar. They will keep you from being at your best." He immediately regretted the statement. How could he retract it without sounding like he was hitting on her?

She frowned and ignored his comment. "If you suggest Abbie should have planned better, I could learn the answer to the question the Hastings brothers have been betting on for the last four months."

"Which is?"

"This muffin is amazing. Do they make them here?"

"Who—there is a bakery about a mile from here." Had she deliberately distracted him? Like a muffin could tempt him to let his diet go. No white flour or sugar. "And the bet?"

"Oh, that too. She bet on how big of a man she could take down while in the family way."

"You bet on that?"

"Nope, only the brothers. I'm sure it's a joke. They have a running list of them. They all doubt she has given up being a bodyguard for good despite Preston's billions. And they are probably right. I think she will say she is just being a mother when she takes down some jerk who gets too close to her kids. I assume you've planned for that in her details." Deidre smoothed the paper muffin wrapper, folded it, then put it on the center of her plate.

"I can't believe her brothers would do that." Even his own brother wouldn't. If his brother knew him well enough. The seven-year age difference created a distance neither of them had tried to bridge.

"You don't know the Hastings very well, do you? The brothers are just as fierce about protecting Abbie as they are about teasing her."

"I guess that's how siblings should be. I don't have any sisters. Do you have any brothers?"

"How do you think I got into martial arts? Polynesian boys all play rugby and grow up to be either rugby or football players. Every one of my brothers ended up with a college scholarship. When I was little, they made me play rugby with them. I always ended up on the losing end of that. After they broke my arm, Mom told me I needed to find a way to defend myself. Then she put me on the couch with my new pink cast and played the original *Karate Kid* movie. Looking back, I think she chose the movie deliberately. When I saw him take on the bigger, stronger guys with that move, I knew karate was what I needed to learn. I begged my father for lessons until he gave in."

Not what Liam had expected. Even as a child she must have been very determined. She had to be to have made it to the world championships. "Did you ever use your skills on them?"

"I tried to power punch my oldest brother after my first lesson. It didn't go so well." Her melodic laughter surprised him. "After a year of lessons, they learned to back off. Then I won my first local title, and I kept on winning, and they became my biggest cheerleaders. Figuratively and literally." Deidre searched her phone for a moment before showing him a photo of her standing in between four large men. They all had to either be standing on stools or over six and half feet tall.

Workers came into the kitchen, and Deidre cleared her dirty dishes.

Liam followed her out of the room to one of the sitting areas.

Deidre sat down in a plush white chair. "So now we spend most of our day waiting?"

"Pretty much. That's the definition of "on call." We still need to work out your sleep schedule." Liam held up his phone.

She gave him another half smile. "I have nothing better to do."

Liam smiled back. Following his father's advice would be easier than he thought.

DEIDRE LOOKED AT THE TIME on her phone and covered her head with her pillow. She was scheduled to sleep for another two hours. Her body wasn't complying with her plan to keep Abbie safe, and yet she wasn't ready to concede to Liam that her eight-awake, eight-asleep plan was fatally flawed. Fifteen minutes later, she tossed the covers off. Six hours of sleep was good enough. And since it was past 7:00 p.m., there might still be some dinner left.

No one sat at the tables, and the warmer held only a few scraps of a chicken dish that had reached the point of being twice cooked. Deidre placed the wilted salad remains on her plate next to the two tablespoons of edible chicken from the bottom of the pan. Were they allowed to cook in the kitchen or only make sandwiches? Her grand sleeping plan hadn't accounted for the fact that she depended on others for her meals.

Liam wandered into the kitchen. "You're up early." He crossed to the fridge and took out a foil-wrapped plate. "I saved you this. I wasn't sure what you liked."

Deidre took the plate from him. She added the salad from it to what was on her plate, as well as a piece of garlic bread, before putting the chicken into the microwave. "Thank you. I was wondering what I was going to do about the food situation."

"I told the cook what you were doing, and she said I could make a plate for you anytime. If you want to cook something yourself, you need to write the food you use on her shopping list. Don't worry about things like the boxed cereal, milk, sandwich fixings, and condiments."

The microwave dinged. Deidre checked her food before removing it. "Thank you for saving me dinner. I didn't even think of eating when I planned this."

Liam took the seat next to her. "Not a problem. I wouldn't be a very good boss if I didn't look out for you."

"Is that what you learned in the military?"

"Not in those words. How are you going to keep yourself awake for the next eight hours?"

"Ten. I need to keep on the schedule. I figured I'd catch up on a bunch of shows I've missed, then go work out when I got tired. By 5:00 a.m., I should be able to sleep until one. I'll eat breakfast before I go to bed. Do you suppose they will have the muffins by then?"

"I don't think so. Would you like me to save you one?"

Could his carb-hating hands handle picking one up? Better not push it. "You don't need to do that."

"It isn't a problem."

"Thanks." Why wasn't he pointing out the stupidity of her plan? Another thing she could do with the ten long hours that lay ahead was puzzle out his kindness tonight.

"I found a gazillion board games. Many of them are two-player. If you want, after dinner, we can play a couple."

Deidre tried to hide her surprise behind her last bite of dinner. Yesterday's stiff, all-business Liam versus today's considerate Liam—which one was real, or were they both false? Well, nothing brought out a person's true personality like getting beat in a heated board game. Too bad she hadn't figured that out years ago. The strategy could have saved her some pain if fifth dates were mandatory game nights. "That sounds like a good way to stay awake. I'll finish my dinner. You choose the first game."

Liam chose Scrabble. Spelling had never come easy for her. One of the primary reasons she had gone to the police academy instead of college was because of her fear of writing papers. Spell-check didn't always help, autocorrecting as it did to a word she never intended to use.

The final score was closer than she expected due to her getting three triple-word scores. When the first round of torture was over, Deidre chose Othello.

"Strategy games?" Liam asked as he set the four center pieces on the board. He was obviously familiar with the game.

"They are my favorite. Less luck involved. Monopoly is a combination of both, which is why with only two players, the game can last for hours."

"What's your favorite game?"

Deidre pondered where to place her third piece. "It changes. I enjoy playing Uno with my brothers and cousins, Clue with my mother, Othello and chess with my father. My grandparents would teach us all sorts of card games with strange names. What's yours?"

"Risk." He laid down a piece, flipping over more than half of hers in one move and opening a corner.

Deidre took the corner. "I should have known. Conquering the world fits you."

"I'm not sure whether I should feel insulted or complimented. I shouldn't have let you have that corner."

Deidre smiled at him as she claimed a second corner, securing an entire side. "Let? I could argue that I lured you into it."

"Hmm. You aren't competitive at all, are you?"

"I think we've already established that I am. I may not have won at the Taekwondo World Championships, but I made it there. Do you consider yourself competitive?"

"I didn't think I was, but looking back, maybe. I always wanted to be like my older brother, so I competed with my version of his shadow." He laid the second to last piece down and shook his head. "Apparently, this is one game I don't compete well in. Best two out of three?"

Deidre turned over the remaining pieces. He'd lost well. Not an ounce of grumbling. Othello was her favorite game of the night.

Liam double-checked the schedule. He should have had the gym to himself since Deidre would be sleeping for another hour, but he'd arrived to find her stretching in the center of the mat.

"Good afternoon." Her stretching made him wince as he thought about forcing his body to move in such a way.

"I didn't mean to intrude on your time."

"You're not. It's a big gym." Deidre moved into the splits.

Was she showing off? Perhaps it was time to see if she was as good as she claimed to be. "We could spar."

"Really?" She hopped up, way too eager.

The corner cabinet held several sizes of gear. Deidre picked a red helmet, gloves, and boots. Liam chose blue.

"Rules?" asked Deidre.

"None?" At her smile, Liam regretted his answer.

They had circled each other for a few seconds when Deidre threw a punch. Liam swung back, and she knocked his arm out of the way, taking him off guard. A sweep of her foot sent him to the mat. Deidre threw herself across his chest, pinning him. "My point."

It wasn't a question.

They got up for a second round. Liam dove for her waist on the first move, taking her to the ground, but she twisted out of his hold. He used his weight to pull her down, and after a moment of wrestling, he pinned her. "My point."

They stood. "Three or five?"

"Five."

Her kick caught him off guard again. Every negative thought

he'd ever had about females in the industry flew out of his head as he was propelled backward. All his moves became defensive—and then he was looking at the ceiling lights, Deidre looming over him. "My point. Sure you want more?"

Liam remained on the mat, catching his breath. "You seem to be having a bit too much fun. I'm going to call this at three."

She gave him a hand up. "I've been waiting for this since we met. I think I'm more motivated."

That may have been *a* factor, but it wasn't *the* factor. She was good, and he hadn't expected it. "I take back everything I said. Other than the rare female who joins the profession to get a man, I have nothing but respect."

"What about the men who join to get a woman?"

"What?"

Deidre removed her helmet. "Some male bodyguards use their job to pick up women. They adore the ones who grab their biceps and blink up at them." She acted out her words, imitating perfectly more than one of the dates he'd been on. "'Flex for me again? Liam, you're so strong.'" Deidre dropped her hands and stepped back. "A bodyguard from a California firm hit on me last February. If I hadn't been masquerading as a helpless secretary, I would have tossed him to the floor."

The look of disgust on her face made him laugh. "I can't picture you acting helpless."

Deidre stored her gear, pulled out her ponytail, ran her fingers through her hair, and turned toward him. Liam blinked. Something in her face was soft, vulnerable. She sauntered over to him, not in a Hollywood-vamp or overdone-prostitute way but something completely feminine, even though she had worked out and still glistened with perspiration. She set her palm on the middle of his chest.

Oh, wow. It burned.

She blinked up at him, eyes wide. "Sir? Can you help me? My car has a flat."

Liam looked for a car. She must have felt his heart speed up.

Deidre stepped back. "Convincing?"

"Do you act often?"

"Occasionally. I've done some undercover. How are you at undercover work?"

"Honestly, I have no idea. I think I will always look and act like me."

Deidre dragged him in front of the mirror. "Let's try something. Slouch a little."

Liam hunched over.

"Not like the Hunchback of Notre Dame. Like you are tired or your girlfriend just told you she likes your roommate better." Deidre adjusted his shoulders and back. "Now, I want you to think about the kid in your high school who knew everything about everything but couldn't hold a conversation with anyone. Be him."

The kid from his science class.

"Look in the mirror. Do you see the change?"

Liam nodded.

"Now, ask me out."

Liam looked at Deidre, then at his shoes. He felt his face flush. The mirror confirmed it. "Would you go to the movies—"

She smiled. He couldn't finish and looked back down at his shoes.

"Perfect!" She threw an arm around him. "You didn't look military or threatening at all."

Liam returned the hug. They froze and stepped back.

"Thanks for the acting lesson."

"Thanks for letting me win the sparring match." Deidre smiled.

"I didn't let you win."

"I know. But I'll never tell. What happens in the gym stays in the gym." She grabbed a towel off the bench and disappeared down the hall.

Liam looked in the mirror and tried to change personas. It didn't matter. Real or imaginary, he couldn't ask her out.

DEIDRE FUMBLED FOR HER PHONE, checking the time and date. One p.m., Saturday.

It was time to admit this experiment wasn't working, even if she had passed the tests Liam had devised. The sleep she was getting wasn't restorative. Spending all her waking hours with Liam while pretending that three sleeps ago there hadn't been a moment when their fun had turned to flirting and almost something more, drained her. During her last awake time, she'd watched enough old romance movies to admit there was a bundle of chemistry between her and Liam. Unfortunately, in their line of work, romance was more hazardous than the animosity that had flowed between them last Saturday when they met.

Her phone screen displayed an unfamiliar alert. Deidre tapped on it, and it took her to the message center of the Dermot Security app.

At hospital. Director called a 12:30 meeting. Decided to not wake you up. Be back at 14:00.

Seriously? She would have only missed an hour of sleep at most. What happened to waking her up for important things? Deidre dressed and went to find her lunch. If he wasn't here, there wouldn't be a covered plate waiting in the fridge, as the cook didn't clear lunch until 1:30, meaning she needed to hurry.

Nothing remained of the mock pasta salad or chicken-cranberry croissant sandwiches. From the freezer, Deidre pulled one of the leftover boxes the cook made for employees who missed a meal or didn't like the day's fare.

Another reason to stop with this ridiculous sleep schedule. She was tired of reheating all her food. And she hadn't gotten one of the good muffins for — She didn't know. She'd lost count. No, she would have had one Friday morning. She had been awake for breakfast, but she'd done a long workout that had included sparring with Liam again. He'd changed his defensive and offensive tactics, the new strategies reminding her of sparring with Adam Hastings the first time as he figured out when she would use a martial-arts technique. Neither of them mentioned the hug from the day before. Deidre rubbed her temples and rechecked the calendar in her phone to make sure she had her days right.

As much as she wanted to prove that her unconventional idea was good, there was no way she would endanger Abbie. The time disorientation left her in a vulnerable place.

After lunch, she wandered into the huge Harmon library and found Abbie sitting in one of the leather recliners. "Hey, stranger. How is your sleep experiment?"

Deidre sat in the nearest seat. "I'm declaring it a failure. For the last sixteen hours, I hoped I was wrong. I don't want an 'I told you so' from Liam. I really hoped eight-hour sleeping would help me be more alert so I could be prepared for the delivery."

Abbie's laugh brightened her tired face. "If preparing for a delivery could only be so easy. I don't think I am getting any sleep. The three of them seem to wrestle for shotgun position. It reminds me of my brothers when I was little. Only now I can't stand back and let them have it out since I'm the boxing ring."

"Ouch."

"It doesn't hurt too much, but every once in a while they use my bladder as a trampoline, and that is annoying."

Another pregnant woman entered the room. She must be Alex's new wife, Kimberly. Deidre had only seen photos and knew she was living on the estate. "I didn't realize you had company. I can come back at a better time."

"Don't go." Abbie pointed to another chair. "Kimberly? Have you met Deidre? She works for Hastings."

Deidre rose to shake hands and was met with an unexpected hug. Someone needed to inform Kimberly not to randomly hug bodyguards. It made them nervous. Like the last hug.

"Sorry, I've been stealing hugs whenever I can, and I've heard so much about you. Both Alex and Abbie talk about your skills all the time. Elle—or do you call her ZoElle?—talks about you too. She wants more training. I'm talking too much, aren't I? Hazard of spending too much time alone."

"I should leave you two to talk." Deidre turned to leave.

"Please stay," said Abbie. "Kimberly is right. I need a good chat, and I imagine you do too."

"I'm on call."

Abbie rolled her eyes. "Look, bodyguard, there have been no contractions, and since I am paying Dermot, and Dermot Security is paying you, I say you can stay. It isn't like they can be upset with you since your job is to protect me and the babies. Unless you have someplace you are supposed to be."

"Liam went to a meeting at the hospital without me, so I am on my own. Just waiting." Deidre raised her footrest like the other women.

"Aren't we all? Of course, Kimberly needs to wait another two months. Look how tiny she is compared to me." Abbie pulled her blouse tight over her bulging middle.

Kimberly did the same with her shirt. "Singleton on board."

Unconsciously, Deidre brought her hand over her empty womb as the other two laughed.

"Who is Liam? The tall man who needs to let his hair grow out?" Kimberly asked, changing the subject.

Abbie answered. "He is Simon Dermot's youngest son. And although Deidre refuses to agree because he is her boss,"—she half covered her mouth and stage whispered—"he is a rather nice piece of eye candy." Abbie dropped her hand. "I'm saying this objectively since you both know I love Preston to pieces, but even in high school, Liam looked fine, and the military helped him mature in some very nice ways."

If Abbie thought he was eye candy, she should see him dripping wet and getting out of the backyard swimming pool. More like death by chocolate. "You knew him back then?"

"Not really. We didn't go to the same school or anything, but when the security companies had their mini Olympic competitions, we'd both be there. He is a couple years older, so it wasn't like he ever noticed me. And he didn't speak much with my brothers either. Opposite teams and all. Back then, I couldn't imagine we would work together. But I don't think I understood the dynamics of large events and multiple clients. I'm not supposed to ask, but how are plans for my protection and the babies' going?"

"If you aren't supposed to ask, I'm probably not supposed to tell you anything. So everything is in hand, and you get to ignore my smiling face the entire labor." Deidre flashed a Cheshire Cat grin. Both women started laughing, holding their baby bumps.

Abbie wiped her eyes. "Please don't grin like that in the delivery room. Laughter hurts. And I absolutely don't want any more pain."

"I'll use this one instead." Deidre used the expressionless face that was as much a part of her uniform as her suit or the blue Hastings Security polo.

Abbie mirrored her.

"How do you do that?" asked Kimberly. "You could both pass for mannequins. It's kind of creepy."

"Practice. A lot. When you are wearing an earpiece and a warning comes over it, no one can know you've heard a thing. The last thing you want is anyone other than the bodyguards reacting. And the principal is not to know about the threat until after the fact, if possible," said Deidre.

"Which brings us back to the hospital plan." Abbie folded her arms and waited.

Deidre dropped the footrest. It was uncomfortable being so relaxed around a client, even with permission. "I've already told you everything—"

"Miss Ross!" Liam's sharp voice echoed through the library.

Deidre stood to face him.

"Now." He didn't need to say more. Deidre hurried from the library to give him a piece of her mind.

Liam led her down the hallway to the employee residences. He opened the door to the blue parlor and shut it behind them. Frustration from the hospital meeting was fueling his reaction, the walk not having calmed him at all. "What do you think you were doing? You have strict orders not to share the hospital plan with the principal."

"I didn't." She stepped into his space, her stance challenging.

"I heard you!"

"No, you didn't. You heard part of a conversation, and now you are jumping to conclusions. I was saying I had already told her everything I could, which, FYI, was the facial expression I would be wearing the entire delivery!"

"You are on duty, and I find you sitting in a recliner!"

Deidre's voice lowered to a deathly calm. "If you had thought to include me in your important meeting at the hospital, I wouldn't have had to look for something to do. And, FYI, Abbie insisted I sit and talk. And since, ultimately, she is paying me to be here 24/7 and she said she was not in labor, I saw no problem with it."

"Your job isn't to decide if there is a problem with acting beyond established protocols."

"Fine, Mr. Boss Man. Whatever you say. Do you have any other unfounded accusations?"

"They are not unfounded. You shouldn't be getting too close to the client. It causes problems."

"I can't ignore her either. We were colleagues. There is a friendship that comes with that. I can't pretend we don't have a connection when I will be standing in a room with her for who knows how many hours in various stages of undress, which may not matter to her during hard labor, but a week later, it will. For her sake, I can't be cold and unfriendly. You can have that job." Deidre turned to leave.

"You are not dismissed." He reached for her arm, but she slapped his hand away.

She turned back and mock saluted him. "Yes, boss. Anything else, boss? Because I would like to go cool off before you inform me of anything else you don't like about my performance. Abbie wouldn't appreciate us brawling in one of her nice rooms, and if you touch me again, I will take you down." She clicked her heels together and saluted again before exiting.

Liam didn't stop her. His phone vibrated. Mrs. Harmon was requesting a meeting with Deidre and him in the library in ten minutes. Great. This close to the delivery, if she fired either of them, her safety would be in question. There might not be time to train a whole new detail, not to mention the issue with locating a competent female bodyguard. And if he went, would his father's firm suffer? Their main client was the Harmons and their business holdings. He ran his hand down his face. There was no way this would turn out well. And he still had to disclose the results of the meeting with the hospital administration. Liam straightened his tie in the mirror hanging over the small fireplace. If only he hadn't been in such a hurry to disclose the results of the meeting. Now he owed

Deidre a huge apology and had tossed the trust he'd been trying to earn.

Deidre had beat him to the library, having changed into workout clothes, no doubt en route to beat up on the sparring dummy. She stayed on Mrs. Harmon's far side.

Mrs. Harmon frowned. "I'm glad to see you are both still alive. I will not lecture you, but I am giving you both the afternoon off. Get away from the estate and each other. My nurse has already been in for her check, and my mother will be here in a half hour." She put her hand to her belly. "These three are under strict orders to stay exactly where they are. Deidre, whatever you do, don't work out again. Relax. My poor sparring dummy needs a rest. Liam, next time you have an issue involving me, I hope you will be polite enough to wait for the punch line before interrupting, unless I am in imminent danger. If you had been patient enough to hear her answer, you would know we were discussing the same passive face you are wearing right now."

"Sorry, ma'am."

Mrs. Harmon's eye roll came with an exaggerated mom sigh. "Well, what are you two doing here? Go!"

Deidre left through the far door, which was closer to the gym. Liam left through the other. He still needed to talk to her about the hospital visit, which he should have woken her up for. The news would change the master delivery plan. Liam opened the Dermot Security app and texted Deidre.

Hospital Administration has cut down our security presence due to HIPAA. We need to rework things. Should he apologize in the text? He pondered before hitting send. Apologies didn't work well in texts. A valuable lesson from his last girlfriend.

—How much?

Major. We are losing the two other guards on the floor.

—Oh.

Liam waited for another response. Four minutes and thirty-five seconds later, he received one.

—By 'we need to rework things,' did you mean you wanted my input?

Yes. Why else would he have written her?

—So much for a Saturday afternoon off.

Did you make plans already?

—If you mean my to-do list, yes, I have plans.

Is three hours long enough?

He waited ninety seconds for the response.

—I can be done in two. Where do you want to meet? I don't dare come back here early. Abbie is mad, and you got an eye roll.

An eye roll was bad? Liam tried to think of a place to meet, short of a five-star restaurant, where Deidre wouldn't fight him. The napkin the cook had written on that morning caught his eye. A quick internet search confirmed the business was open until eight on Saturdays. If it was too busy, they could move someplace else.

I'll send you an address. See you at 16:00.

—K

Liam checked his watch. Hopefully, two hours and twenty-one minutes was enough time for her to cool off and for him to sort out his apology.

ALL HER PLANTS STILL LIVED despite Fiona not watering them. It had only been ... Deidre counted on her fingers. Five days? Yes, five. The sleeping thing was so not working. Plus, she was a total crab, worse than PMS crabby. Theoretically, she wasn't sleep-deprived. She had threatened to take her boss down. She was lucky he wasn't firing her. Probably the only reason he would keep her on was, as Abbie pointed out, that ultimately, Abbie had the last say in who stood guard during the delivery. Meaning they were stuck with each other.

She could do this. *At least when I tried, he wasn't a jerk*. Deidre checked through her closet for anything else she might need. Her old swimming suit wasn't as nice as the one she had ordered from a shop downtown and delivered to the mansion, so she left it.

Twenty minutes and her errands were done. Only an hour and a half to kill. Deidre sat in front of the TV, surfing for an end-of-season rugby game or anything to keep her mind off Liam. An ad for the US Army came on. She changed the channel and landed in the middle of an ad for the Marines. Seriously, it was Saturday-afternoon sports. It was supposed to be all beer ads.

The front door opened, and Fiona came in with three grocery bags. "Deidre, what are you doing here? You didn't get fired in less than a week, did you?"

"Have a little faith. I am on a mandatory afternoon break. My boss and I got into it, and I needed a breather."

"Your boss, as in last week's disaster date?"

"Pretty much."

"See, you are perfect for each other."

"What part of 'we got into a fight' did you miss? If it weren't for Abbie, I'd demand a transfer."

"It takes sparks to make a fire. And I know I saw sparks last Saturday."

"You are imagining things." Sparks in the gym? Definitely. A warm glow when he remembered she needed to eat? Yep. But Fiona didn't need to know about those things.

"You may not have noticed, but I did. How many men have you met who were rude about your profession or assumed you were weak?"

"No idea. Fifty to a hundred?"

"How many of them did you want to strangle?"

Deidre saw where Fiona was going with her questions and tried to evade them. "A small handful."

"And of those men, how many did you end up dating?"

"All but one."

Fiona's eyebrows went up. "Which one?"

"My current boss. Note the word *boss* equals not happening. Not now, not ever."

"I think she doth protest too much." Fiona tossed a small pillow at Deidre.

"Not really. You should have seen us this afternoon. I wanted nothing more than to land his butt in the middle of a sparring mat, and he was nearly as mad as I've seen a man get."

"Did he hit you?"

"No."

"Kiss you?"

"You are seriously crazy."

"Good. Then you can take physically abusive off your list. I'd say 90 percent sure he is not."

"Still my boss." Deidre threw the pillow back at Fiona.

"Can you look me in the eye and tell me you feel zero attraction to him?"

"It doesn't matter if I do or not. You are making this situation more difficult. I don't need to analyze my attraction to him."

"So you are attracted. Say his name." Fiona stood in front of Deidre, blocking her on the couch. Not that she was an obstacle, but she wasn't in danger—a fact Fiona used to her advantage.

Deidre used her at-work face and calm voice. "Liam."

Fiona frowned. "Not fair. I can't see your true reaction when you do that."

"Are you done yet? I know you think this is funny, but it's not. If Abbie went into labor at this very moment, the fact that we are angry at each other could endanger her. I need to be able to get along with him and *not* as a love interest. Attraction is dangerous. I need to get us to be coworkers with mutual respect. We have both been working on this all week. I'm pretty sure he let me win a round of Risk just so we could get along. Like I let him win at Clue. Although with two people, the game isn't much of a challenge. Now we are back at five days ago when neither of us trusted the other. I can't let anything happen to Abbie and her babies because I'm having difficulty with Liam or I'm wondering if that flash of attraction was two-way. I can't do that. Don't ask me to."

Fiona sat next to her. "I didn't realize. I thought since he wasn't your coworker…"

"After the babies are born, you can tease me about any guy you want to, but Liam is off-limits right now. I need to figure out how to be a good coworker after the things I said today."

"What did you say?"

"Hopefully not half of what I was thinking. But I did threaten him."

Pulling a pillow into her lap, Fiona leaned back. "I could be wrong, but in your industry, having the guts to physically take your boss out may not be a bad thing. He could respect that you are willing to stand up."

Only Fiona could think that. "I hope you are right. I need to go meet him now."

"I thought you had the afternoon off."

"I do as far as Abbie is concerned. Not so much when it comes to Liam."

"Good luck. And I promise I'll water your plants." Fiona's half hug gave Deidre the courage to drive to the address Liam gave her—the bakery that made the cranberry muffins she liked. Interesting meeting place. Liam must be hoping to smooth over their altercation this afternoon. Deidre parked her car in one of several empty spots, took five deep, cleansing breaths, and went in.

When the bell over the door rang, Liam did not need to look up to see who'd entered. Deidre's car had come into the parking lot long enough ago that he wondered if she was having second thoughts. He was.

She sat down next to him as the position gave her the second-best view of the room. "Are you trying to bribe me?"

"Not sure. Do you still want to hit me?"

"I need to apologize for that. And by the way, the eight-hour thing isn't working. I haven't been this irrationally upset in a very long time."

"I wouldn't call you irrational. I was yelling at you for something you didn't do. I'm sorry I jumped to conclusions. I know you wouldn't endanger Mrs. Harmon."

"Can we consider the apology phase of this meeting over with?"

"Are you sure you want to? I was going to offer you an apology muffin."

"Oh, in that case, I'll wait a few seconds for you to finish groveling."

"Do you want to choose one? They have more flavors than the cranberry orange walnut you've been hoarding all week."

He stood, tempted to pull Deidre's chair out for her the way his grandmother insisted, but she beat him to it. They went to stand in front of the glass case.

"This was a mistake. I want one of everything. Apple, raspberry, and look at the savory ones." Deidre pointed to almost everything in the case. "So your plan was to bring me here so I would eventually eat enough to slow me down?"

"I hadn't thought of that. I guess I shouldn't mention they have brownies and cookies too."

Deidre glanced sideways at him. "You do realize it might be called evil to tempt me like this."

An employee hovered behind the counter.

Deidre closed her eyes and pointed. "I choose that one."

"Apple crunch is one of our best sellers. And you, sir?"

Liam chose a low-carb, gluten-free option and paid for both muffins. Deidre filled the complementary water cups.

Only one other customer sat in the store, wearing earbuds. Liam pulled out his tablet. "They are only going to allow us a maximum of three guards on the floor at any one time. One in the room, one outside the door, and one at the nursery window after the babies arrive. We can have a five-minute change of the guard. Preston Harmon's guards will only be allowed in the waiting room when he is there and no further. The same for his parents. We may have an inconspicuous presence in the main lobby on the first floor. And our request to find out if there are any unexpected patients has been denied."

"I thought they had already approved your four-man plan."

"The hospital lawyers got nervous about the possibility of HIPAA violations and lawsuits. The legal team was quick to point out they have never had a baby mix-up or kidnapping."

"What about the Hastings? Did they put any limit on them?"

"No, they are family. But they do have a family visitor limit of three in the waiting room and three in the delivery room. You, Mrs. Harmon, and Preston Harmon will be those three."

"Hastings like to stay busy, and we know Jethro will be there. Give them jobs. They can rotate out of the waiting room."

"They won't be able to get past the doors into the maternity ward until they have permission after the birth, so they'll only have eyes on other visitors and the main elevator. The patient elevator and other families will be out of their purview, so they will be of little use."

"I never thought I would see the day I could say having a Hastings around would be useless." Deidre covered her mouth. "Don't ever tell them I said that."

"I'll chalk it up to your sleep pattern."

"I don't know what to do. I was hoping to always be refreshed."

"Take a siesta."

"What do you mean?"

"Have a regular 16/8 day but take a two-hour rest after lunch. You don't need to sleep, just completely relax. How are you at twenty-minute power naps?"

"Not very good. I take all twenty minutes to fall asleep."

"I can show you some relaxation techniques I've learned to deal with that. Also, I think we should both take more breaks. As long as we are in a fifteen-minute radius of the estate-to-hospital route, we should be good."

"What about the hospital?" Deidre popped the last bite of muffin into her mouth.

"Your plan doesn't change. The outside-door guard is going to have to walk a ten-by-ten to see down either hallway. I don't see that we have many options."

"The hospital security will have their cameras manned?"

"They claim they always do."

Deidre folded her muffin wrapper into a square. "Will they warn us if they see something?"

"*If* they do."

"I don't like the sound of that *if*." Deidre's phone buzzed in unison with his.

Mrs. Harmon en route to hospital.

Deidre said the word he was thinking.

Liam dropped a ten on the table, and they ran for their cars.

The babies can't come today. It's much too early! The thought ran like a song on repeat through Deidre's mind as she followed Liam's car. There was nothing else to do but respond, follow the plan, and pray the contractions subsided.

Only Deidre hadn't prayed since the last time she'd prayed for a child who'd come too soon.

Would God hear her?

She didn't know. But he'd better be listening to Melanie and Jethro. At a stoplight still a mile from the hospital, Deidre said the only prayer she could think of. "Please, God, not Abbie. Don't let her suffer such pain."

The phone vibrated twice. Deidre ignored the messages. Her first job was to arrive at the hospital safely. She found a space in the patient-and-visitor lot and checked the Dermot app before running into the building.

Admitting via emergency bay. Moving her to maternity.

Arrived on maternity floor. Mrs. Hastings is with them. Check in at nurses' station for your passes.

Deidre pocketed her phone and checked for her gun. The special permit signed by the hospital administration was in the pocket of her holster, along with her carry permits. She exited her car the same time as Liam. He carried a small box. They jogged across the lot.

In the elevator, Liam opened the box. "Earpieces?"

Deidre took one and placed it in her ear. "Testing one, Deidre."

A voice she didn't know came through the radio. "We have you, Deidre."

"Testing two, Liam."

"We have you, Liam," the same voice confirmed.

The doors opened. "We are on-site." Liam's voice echoed with the split-second delay between what he was saying next to her and what she heard through the earpiece. Deidre recognized the bodyguards standing in the waiting area. Liam went to speak with them. Deidre picked up the phone on the wall next to the maternity ward's locked door. "Deidre Ross. Clearance 1852."

The door buzzed, and Deidre entered the ward. A nurse at the desk checked Deidre's photo ID before sending her to the back-corner room. Was it a good sign Abbie wasn't in the delivery room? Deidre slipped through the door and waited behind the curtain long enough to be sure Abbie wasn't in the middle of being examined before making her presence known. The nurse, one she'd met on an earlier tour, explained the fetal heart monitors. Deidre moved to the corner, where she would be out of the way.

Dr. Song hurried into the room. Deidre listened carefully, trying to process only the information she needed to do her job. Preterm labor and methods for stopping contractions were discussed. Good. Delivery wasn't imminent.

Please make something work. The silent prayer Deidre sent up was all she could do.

The doctor ordered an IV and the appropriate medication.

Deidre went into the hall to report. "Probable preterm labor. We are on a wait and see."

"Thanks." Liam's voice came from the hallway to her left. She waited near the door for him to come to her. "What's the medical plan?"

"Stop the contractions. Best guess, we will be here at least until morning. It depends on how she responds. Mrs. Hastings is with her, and one nurse, who is watching the monitors. Preston is there too."

"Do you need to be in the room?"

"Not as long as it's only the four of them, with or without the doctor. There is nothing to watch that can't be observed from out here. The doctor will check in an hour to see how things are going."

Liam checked his watch. "Take forty minutes to get dinner and whatever else you can. When you get back, we can reassess."

"They are only going to allow one of us in the hallway, right?"

"Yes, but with no activity in the room, now is a good time for you to be prepared."

"What about you?"

"I can spell off with one of Preston's guards. They are in the cafeteria. I needed to move them out of the waiting room."

"I'll be back in forty, then, providing the food is edible."

When she stepped off the elevator for the cafeteria, there was a sign pointing in the opposite direction for the chapel. Deidre followed the second sign. No one was in the small room. The stained-glass window was illuminated from behind with electric lights. The colors didn't depict religious symbols beyond rising heavenward.

Deidre sat down on the far back bench and bowed her head. *Please. Please.*

Fifteen hours after he arrived at the hospital, Liam followed the Harmon's service car back to the estate. While everyone was relieved the contractions had been abated, Liam couldn't help but wonder if the stress of his and Abbie's fight had helped bring them on. Even if he asked, the answer would be one the doctor couldn't know. He parked in his spot in the underground garage hidden beneath the main garage. Deidre parked next to him. He waited for her before walking to the house. They both stifled yawns.

"I know we need to analyze what needs to change." Liam covered his mouth to hide another yawn. "However, unless you saw a critical gap, I vote we table the discussion for the next several hours."

"You'll need a way to sleep. Perhaps a van in the parking lot. It won't change my role, but the rest of the detail needs to be able to spell each other off." Her sentence also ended with a yawn. "Neither of us slept enough for it to count in the waiting-room chairs."

"Good idea. I'll put in a request for a van or something."

"Make sure it has an AC unit that can run when the van is parked. Summer in Chicago and all."

Liam held the employee door open. "Maybe some sort of small RV would work. The far section of the parking lot has a couple dozen spaces for them."

"That would also allow an extra team to be on-site since they have limited our presence in the hospital."

Breakfast was over. The cook had left them a note on the refrigerator informing them the breakfast casserole she'd made was best reheated on medium. Deidre set the note back on the counter and took a pen out of her pocket. On the bottom of the note, she scribbled her thanks and signed both their names.

While the food warmed, Liam texted the office staff his thoughts on an RV large enough for two to sleep while two others sat. He reread the text. AC was mentioned three times. Without correcting the error, he sent the message.

Deidre finished her meal. "So much better than hospital food. Although, surprisingly, it was not terrible. Which reminds me. I won't know when my breaks come, and they probably won't be long. I'll need a few protein bars or drinks I can guzzle in a hurry. I don't know how I missed meals in the plan. The breaks are there but not the food."

Liam typed into his phone. "Got it." He cleared his plate. "Sleep well …"

Deidre stopped at the doorway. "You too. And for the record, I think we made a good team up there."

"It would be completely inappropriate to thank Mrs. Harmon for giving us this fire-drill moment, but I am glad we had it."

Deidre nodded. "Good night. Or afternoon or whatever."

Liam laughed, and Deidre returned it. Hers was one of those melodic laughs that made him want to tell her jokes just to hear it again. When the babies arrived, they could celebrate with a date to a comedy club.

feet under him in the five-foot-deep pool, the water sloshing over him, he heard laughter replace the sound of the pumps.

"You did that deliberately!" Liam splashed water at Deidre, drenching her.

"Oh!" She jumped up. "Careful of the electronics."

Liam beckoned. "Then come here."

From a corner five feet away, Deidre shook her head, clutching her middle to contain her laughter. "Not on your life."

Liam climbed out, dripping on the cement floor and blocking her in. He took a step toward her. Deidre didn't have enough room to get around him, but there was still enough for her to get in one of the powerful kicks he'd watched her deliver to the sparring dummy. She held up a hand to stop him, her laughter still dancing around them. Liam grabbed her wrist and yanked her to him. Deidre slammed into his body, but he held firm, keeping them both standing, then wrapped his arms around her to incapacitate her. She fit him perfectly—her height, her curves. She hadn't delivered a single punch, but he could have sworn she had as he struggled to keep his breathing normal.

Deidre stopped laughing, then blinked at him, her pupils dilating. Her lips were so close.

As Liam leaned in, Deidre pushed against his chest and ducked under his slackened arm, bringing him back to his senses. She had more sense than he did.

"I'm not going to spar with you here. Too dangerous. I'll be back in a half hour to use the pool." Deidre picked up a towel and hurried out of the room.

What just happened? Or didn't? After drying off, Liam used his towel to mop up the water he'd splashed over the side of the spa. He needed a cold shower and a clear head more than he needed another workout.

What was that? Deidre wasn't stupid. She knew what attraction felt like. What was worse was that she'd wanted to kiss him. Not good. Not good. Not good. The water from the showerhead splashed over her face. They had only known each other for two weeks. Two days ago they were fighting. There had to be a middle ground where they could coexist.

As she lathered up her hair, a song from an old musical came to mind, and she began singing it at the top of her lungs. As she was rinsing, she remembered that washing a man out of her hair hadn't worked for the woman in the musical, who'd ended up marrying the guy she was trying to get rid of. Deidre stopped singing.

If only they could spend a day or two apart or have a third person on the detail to help balance things out. Neither would happen. The protection plan didn't account for anyone extra on the detail.

Her cell phone rang as she exited the shower. The call went to voice mail. *Kui* Vuki. Raised in Tonga, Grandma Vuki insisted all her grandchildren learn a bit of the language. Deidre called her grandmother back. "*Malo e lelei,* Kui. I am sorry I didn't answer. I was in the shower."

"You should be here today for our feast. Your father is cooking *puaka tunu*. My friend's grandson will be here, and he is very handsome."

Deidre's mouth watered at the mention of the roast pig. Kui setting her up was not so appetizing. "I'm sorry, Kui, I am working today. I explained to Mom already. I can't leave Chicago for Memorial Day."

"You are guarding a pregnant woman. She doesn't need a bodyguard to have a baby. She needs a midwife." Kui's English still carried her island accent. Occasionally, she dropped a word.

Putting her grandma on speakerphone, Deidre dressed while they talked.

"I know, Kui, but because her husband is so wealthy, there is a concern someone might try to kidnap one of the babies or take photos and sell them to the tabloids."

"Hmph. You should be here, feasting with us and meeting a nice island boy, not one of those pasty Americans. Look what the last one brought you. Heartache."

Deidre refrained from telling Kui about her friends who had married islanders whose marriages hadn't worked out. She also didn't point out that her mother was one of those "pasty" Americans. For some reason, Kui thought mom was an islander stuck in the wrong body and accepted her wholeheartedly. "When the time is right, I will look for another husband."

"You need to find a good man. A strong man who will make you happy."

The image of Liam in his swimsuit came to mind unbidden, muscles in all the right places. Deidre changed the subject. "Who's making the yams?"

"Hmph."

Obviously not Grandma.

"If you came, you could have helped me make them, and I wouldn't be stuck making rice." Kui's voice sounded like her four-year-old niece's when the boys wouldn't let her play.

"You forget, Kui. I was the one who burned them two years ago."

"Oh yes, maybe it's better you don't cook. But your cakes are good."

Deidre slipped her shoes on. "Betty Crocker. They come from a box."

"I won't tell. Will you do something fun today?"

"The staff is having a barbecue by the pool this afternoon." Oh, heavens. Liam in a swimsuit again. Maybe she shouldn't go.

"Well, you have fun. Maybe you can come for the Fourth of July."

"I'll try my best. Love you, Kui."

"I love you too."

Deidre went in search of a new book, or in the case of the estate's library, an old book she'd never heard of.

AS THE TIME SLOWLY PASSED, Liam was thankful each day was as uneventful as the last. The entire staff kept track of the pregnancy on the calendar in the kitchen. It had been a week since the preterm labor took Mrs. Harmon to the hospital. Week thirty-three had begun. Every time his phone beeped, he jumped.

Routine helped. Workout, breakfast, review the plans, lunch, siesta, read, dinner, play another board game with Deidre. Repeat.

It was Deidre's night to choose the game. She set a yellow box on the table. "Ever play this one?"

"Pig Mania? Never heard of it."

"It looks like the purpose is to use the pigs as dice."

"That may be why I've never heard of it."

The game went quickly. Liam put the box away. "Movie?"

"Sure. Nothing too suspenseful after the last one. I spent the night trying to catch the bad guy in hyperspeed."

"Rom-com?"

Deidre shook her head. "What about a classic? Cary Grant?"

"John Wayne?"

"Jimmy Stewart?"

"Done!" Liam searched on the actor's name. "Choose a number."

"Nine."

Liam selected the ninth movie on the list. "*The Shop around the Corner?*"

"Never seen it. I think *You've Got Mail* is based on it." Deidre grabbed the throw pillow from the corner of the couch and sat in her usual spot.

Liam sat on the other end, a throw pillow between them. Just like every night, the movie wasn't half over before Deidre fell asleep, curling up in a ball on her end of the couch. Liam sped the movie up to time and a half, knowing if he turned the movie off, she would wake up and want to watch the end. But if he sped it up until the final credits, she'd wake up and go to bed, claiming she'd heard the entire thing.

"Why are they talking so fast?" Deidre's voice startled him.

Liam returned the speed to normal. "The show seemed slow, so I decided to speed it up some."

"You do that all the time. Even on the action shows. Arnold Schwarzenegger is funny fast. Why do you do that?"

"You noticed?"

Deidre sat up and put the pillow back in the corner of the couch. She didn't respond to his question.

"If I stop the movie after you fall asleep, you wake up and want to watch the rest of it. I discovered if I speed it up that you don't. I figured you get more sleep this way. I thought my trick worked the other night. Obliviously it didn't."

Covering her mouth, she started to giggle, which morphed into a full laugh. When it subsided, she said, "I thought I was playing the movies fast in my dream. Such a relief to know I wasn't imagining it. I didn't know your movies could do that."

"I don't think most systems do. This seems to be some sort of prototype." Liam handed her the remote.

"That's the Ogilvie logo. I am often assigned to Mrs. Ogilvie's details. Colin is always inventing things."

The closing credits flashed across the screen. "Mrs. Ogilvie is the one with all the wigs, right?"

"She stands out in a crowd, doesn't she? The kids in the cancer wards love it. She wears the most outrageous ones to the hospitals."

Liam turned off the television. "Mr. Hastings said you don't like hospitals."

Her answer wasn't immediate. "Children's hospitals are different. They paint them bright colors and try to make them as fun as possible. For the most part, I am in the common areas, which look much like modern elementary schools or day cares."

"They should do that for adults."

"I think they try to make them feel more like hotel rooms. They get the same bad art prints."

She hadn't answered the question he thought he asked, but he was enjoying the conversation too much. "How did you get into this business? You aren't former military."

"Former police department. The pay is better, and Hastings treats their employees well. I have never had a problem with any of the harassment or gender issues I experienced with the Chicago PD."

Ouch. He hoped she hadn't seen him wince in the dim lighting. "Have I apologized enough for my behavior the first time we met? I was wrong to have judged everyone on a few bad examples."

"You've been a pretty decent boss, and I think I've given you a different perspective. "

"Dad wants to hire more females, but so few are qualified."

"That's one reason Hastings has training classes. We do general self-defense classes, and every now and then we have a student who's interested in a new career path. Even the women from military or police backgrounds need training in close-combat techniques."

"What will you do after this?" Bodyguards often retired in their early forties.

Deidre shrugged. "I once thought I'd retire and do the soccer- or rugby-mom thing. Maybe I'll consult or move on to the desk part of the job."

"Are you still interested in the mom thing?"

"Yes and no. What about you?"

"I'd like to have a family someday. That's part of the reason I retired from the military. I couldn't keep a long-distance relationship going. I wanted more than just my unit to be my family. I also wanted to be there for my kids. As cute as those videos of Mom or Dad coming home from deployment and surprising their kid are, it isn't the same as having Dad at every school play and Little League game."

"I suppose not. How big of a family do you want?"

"Growing up with only the one brother who was so much older than I was, I thought I'd like three or four children, with not too big of an age gap. But after watching one of my buddies and his wife deal with infertility, I'd be happy with anything."

Deidre covered a yawn. "I think I should go to bed. Night."

Liam stared at the empty doorway, wondering why she'd faked the yawn.

At Abbie's insistence, the Hastings weekly training session was moved to the estate gym. Deidre stood in front of the group of Hastings Security female employees and recruits, leading them through a series of seemingly pointless exercises. In fact, several of the exercises had only one point—to see who would whine or quit. Three of the women were first-time recruits on a five-day trial. Two were in their second month of training and were assigned to supervised details or as building security. The remaining three had been working for at least a year on personal protective details. Only Elle was missing today, as she'd been pulled on to her first major detail involving credible threats.

One recruit made a face and rolled her eyes after a round of jumping jacks. Deidre nodded to Tonie, who had been with Hastings almost as long as Deidre. Tonie gave her a thumbs up.

"Tonie will lead you through several flexibility stretches. This isn't a test but a gauge that'll tell me how much I can put you through without injuring you today."

No one needed to be an Olympic gymnast, yet if they didn't have a certain amount of flexibility, a close protection detail was probably not in their future. However, this flexibility test was more about the disposition of the three new recruits. As she suspected, the one who'd rolled her eyes was the least flexible of the three.

Tonie finished.

"Get your water now." The eye roller was the only one not to follow instructions.

Deidre addressed the recruits. "I need to know what background you have in self-defense."

Eye Roll stepped in front of the others. "Have a black belt."

"In what?"

"Martial arts."

"Which ones?"

Eye Roll struggled. "What my gym taught."

Apparently her gym hadn't done too good of a job teaching the respect side of martial arts. Deidre moved to the next woman. "What background do you have?"

The shortest woman showed humility and some potential. "Not much. I've done the Hastings self-defense workshops. Street fighting with my brothers. But I'd like to learn more."

Deidre turned to the last woman and raised an eyebrow rather than ask again.

"I was enlisted in the army, ma'am. I've had their basic defense training and some close-quarters combat training. I received an honorable discharge after two years because I developed allergies to several foods, including peanuts." A credible reason. Alan would check her story.

Deidre opened the cabinet, counting the sparring equipment. "All three of you have sparred before, right? I'd like to see you in action—"

The door to the gym opened, and Liam entered, causing more of a stir than Deidre would have liked. His reason for ignoring the sign on the door had better be stellar. "Mr. Dermot, did you need something?"

"I'm sorry to interrupt. May I have a moment?"

Deidre nodded at Tonie to take over and followed Liam out into the hall. Liam held his phone. "Mrs. Harmon wanted to see your group before you left. But two of the quick background checks raised red flags. I would have thought the Hastings's check was more thorough."

"There are three new recruits in there, one of whom I will recommend be dismissed today. FYI, don't hire the one in the purple shirt. As far as checks, I'm not sure where Alan was on those."

Liam handed her his phone. Miss Eye Roll's photo came up. The notation showed they had expelled her from college for running an examination cheating ring. The other photo was of Tonie. The accompanying note highlighted a sealed juvenile record. "I'm not surprised about the first one. Abbie knows more about Tonie's history than I do. However, I know they have cleared her, and she has a clean work record."

"I will check with Mrs. Harmon about Tonie today. I can't allow the other woman into the residence."

"I wouldn't want you to. Since Abbie doesn't know any of the recruits, you can leave them here with me while the others go see her."

Liam pocketed his phone. "Works for me. Estate security wants eyes on them." He nodded to one of the estate guards standing at the end of the hall.

"Go clear Tonie. That will only leave you one to worry about." Deidre returned to the gym.

"Who was that? Do you work with him?" The questions came from Miss Eye Roll.

"I think it's time for your first bodyguard-etiquette lesson. First, I am on an active assignment, as Tonie explained before coming here. Two, the estate is under the protection of Dermot Security, not Hastings. That means any information they give me is on a need-to-know basis. If Mr. Dermot needed everyone in this room to know something, he would not have pulled me out into the hall. Third, our client's privacy is of the utmost importance. We don't share anything about our assignments outside of our details other than up line or to Mr. Hastings, Mr. Adam, Mr. Alan, Mr. Alex, and Mr. Andrew, as assigned." Deidre looked each woman in the eye. "As far as Mr. Dermot, his is a face you will want to learn as we often cross over details. You will give him the respect you would give any of the Hastings."

The youngest of the women raised her hand. "I'm confused. Why do you refer to the Hastings by Mr. and their first name?"

"Having five Mr. Hastings gets very confusing. We use *mister* to show respect. We refer to our clients as Mr. or Mrs. My current client was once a coworker and is still a friend. At her request, I use her first name, even when I'm on call. If I were on an active protective detail, I would say Mrs. Harmon over the comms, our communication devices, or in a detail meeting, unless there were a designated code name."

"Should we call you Ms. Ross?"

"Not unless I am leading your detail. Now for sparring. Let's pair you up." Deidre paired an experienced guard with each of the recruits and the two trainees against each other and rotated them through. Liam returned during Tonie's round with Miss Eye Roll. Tonie took the round easily.

"Clean up. I'll be back in five." Deidre left the room with Liam.

"You were right. Tonie is cleared. I sent what we found about the other woman over to Alan. He hadn't found the test scam, but he had found a couple other items. She isn't to leave the gym without an escort. Alan apologized for not finding the information sooner."

"The ones who can go visit will be ready in a couple minutes. Does estate security want someone in the room with her other than just me?" Deidre wondered what to do to keep the three women busy.

"Alan is sending a car. He wants your new recruit gone too. Car will be here in five."

Deidre nodded and returned to the gym. Most of the women didn't take notice of her return.

"I only lost because I was so distracted by that man. Seriously, how can you guys stand working around such hot men all the time?"

Deidre did her own eye roll as she waited for Tonie's answer.

"The fastest way to get yourself fired is to flirt with the men on your detail, and dating within your detail is forbidden. It's too easy to think about your love interest first and your principal second. And breakups make the work situation worse."

"So we can't date any of them?"

Deidre stepped forward. "Dating within the agency is allowed as long as you have filed the proper form with HR. It's a safety precaution. Same as police departments. Mr. and Mrs. Hastings once worked together, so dating is a possibility. However, I advise extreme caution."

"What about guys from other companies?" Miss Eye Roll looked at the other recruits. "Dermot has some hot guys. I'd love to get to know the one you were talking to."

"I think—" Deidre was interrupted by Liam's arrival with one of the Dermot estate details and a Hastings driver. "I think it's time to leave. The three of you are going back to Hastings." Deidre indicated for them to follow the driver. "Mrs. Hastings wants to say hello to the rest of you."

The estate guard nodded at Tonie and the others. "If you'll follow me."

Eye Roll stood with hands on hips. "You didn't answer my question."

"I think if you're looking for a date, this isn't the right career path." Deidre herded her to the door with the others.

"But would you date him if you could?"

"It's time to go." Deidre hoped her dark skin hid any blush as the three finally left.

Liam leaned against the doorjamb. "What was that about?"

"Nothing much. A woman neither of us will hire wants to date bodyguards."

"So, what's your answer to her last question?" Liam's smile sent tingles down her spine.

"That should be obvious." Deidre picked up the last of the workout towels. "You're my boss. I don't date my bosses." Deidre hurried for her room, hoping he didn't realize she still hadn't answered the question. Would she date him if she could? She couldn't let herself think about her answer.

"BOREDOM COMES FROM WITHIN." WHOEVER coined that bit of wisdom had never been on call for weeks on end. Liam checked June 10th off his calendar. Another day as uneventful as the last three. Mrs. Harmon's doctor did a house call rather than have her come into the office. Liam didn't begrudge the choice. It saved the security team and the doctor's office a headache, and a home visit kept Mrs. Harmon from exerting herself. But he hadn't been off the estate grounds for over a week. Yes, he had good food, exercise, and good conversation when Deidre was around.

Part of the problem was that she was always around. Occasionally, another employee would come into the dining room, or one of the estate guards would check in with him. But that was not enough. He was dreaming about Deidre almost nightly, and not work-related dreams. In them, she was sharing his side of the couch or laughing with him over the antics of a dark-haired toddler. He was dreaming about a future—one she'd pointed out wasn't likely to happen since he was her boss.

Since the day of her training class, Deidre had avoided personal discussions. Avoiding each other completely was almost impossible. They sparred together and played several more board games. Deidre had chosen Chutes and Ladders last night. No strategy was involved, and seeing her slip down that long slide was especially fun.

She would take part in discussions on work-related topics, including the hypothetical. *How would you protect a principal in a bank robbery? How would you protect a principal from a space invasion?* And she had several good tips on recruiting more females. The free self-defense seminars not only helped the community, they yielded potentials. But the second any conversation turned even the slightest bit personal, including favorite memories of a pet, Deidre disappeared.

Liam turned his light off and climbed into bed, hoping Deidre was wise enough to stay out of his dreams. He needed to focus on his job.

June 13. The calendar couldn't move slower if time went in reverse. Calendars everywhere mocked her, including the one on the swim-spa controls. Deidre selected her workout and entered the pool. The longer she was bored out of her mind, the better for Abbie. The siestas were much more restful than the eight and eight she'd tried, an added bonus being that she had removed over fifty books from her to-be-read list. Besides nap times, Liam had adjusted their sleeping schedules so he was sleeping from 1:00 a.m. until 9:00 a.m., while she slept from 9:00 p.m. to 5:00 a.m. They worked out together in the afternoon after her siesta and before his. Now on full bed rest, Abbie was keeping the contractions at bay with the help of an in-home nurse.

Deidre neared the end of her morning swim routine. If she ever had the money, she was going to purchase a swim spa. The pumps slowed, and she flipped over for slow backstroke.

Something in the room moved, and she stood and lost her footing in the same movement. Even underwater, she could hear Liam's laugh. Without sputtering, she stood and pushed her hair out of her face. "Were you trying to give me a heart attack?"

"No, I couldn't sleep, so I thought I'd come run on a treadmill. The payback was a coincidence."

The water pumps quit on their own as the workout ended. Deidre climbed out of the spa and wrapped up in a towel. She wished she had a big fluffy robe to cover herself.

Liam turned to the mat. "Do you want to spar?"

"Not this morning. Abbie's doctor wants another ultrasound, and I need to be there a half hour before her."

"I thought the doctor was coming to the house." Liam set his water bottle and towel down and pulled out his phone. "When did you get assigned? Can't they change it?"

"I got the text right before I went to bed. I thought you would know. And, no, they can't assign anyone else because a man would look stupid hanging out in the lobby of an OBGYN office. And I'm pretty much the only one who can be called to the back once the Harmons arrive."

Liam reddened. "Good point. I must still be tired. I didn't think that through before I said it."

Deidre stopped toweling off to look at him. "Are you okay?"

"I'm not used to sitting around doing nothing. I finished Hamilton's biography last night, and I think we've played half the games in the collection."

"That must be hard. But you didn't see action every day in the military, did you?"

"Thank heavens, no. But we always had an assignment. There was always something needing to be done."

"If you think you are bored, imagine Abbie. A year ago, she had a challenging undercover assignment. Now she has to spend twenty-plus hours a day in bed. The last two days, she had a *Pride and Prejudice* marathon. She invited every female who works on the grounds to stop by the theater room on their break for cucumber sandwiches and to vote on the best Mr. Darcy. She even played the Bollywood version."

"How many versions are there?"

"At least eight or nine, including zombies, which is an abomination." Deidre checked the time. "I need to get going. Are you on the detail today?"

Liam searched on his phone. "No. Preston's detail is taking care of Mrs. Harmon's appointment as far as chauffeuring, etc. I guess that's why it fell off my radar."

"When I get back, I'll race you around the perimeter of the estate."

"You're on. I'll win this time."

"Maybe." Deidre waved as she left the room.

THEY ROUNDED THE LAST BEND in the mile-long trail that circled the estate and headed for the designated end point—the gazebo. Liam picked up his speed to pass Deidre, who'd kept a five-yard lead most of the last lap. She sped up too. For the third time in two weeks, she reached the gazebo first.

Liam bent over with his hands on his knees. "How do you do that?"

Deidre walked a circle around him. "Either practice running from four brothers or the fact I eat carbs."

"I'll take the brothers over the carbs."

"Never underestimate the power of a good muffin."

Liam shook his head. They both drank from their water bottles. It was one of those hot mid-June days that felt more like July. "I don't think I do. Long-term, the muffin will get you."

"One of these days you'll realize there is more to life than diet and exercise."

Moving to the shade of the gazebo, Liam sat down. He patted the seat next to him. "I think you have my priorities mixed up. I know there is more ahead for me in life, which is why I eat this way. So I can live it."

"And what are you going to say years from now when your daughter invites you to her three-year-old tea party and wants to serve you cake?"

"She won't eat cake. She won't even know what cookies are."

Deidre rolled her eyes. "So she won't go to preschool, have friends, or watch television?"

"Of course she will."

"I have two words for you: Cookie Monster."

"Point taken. But I don't need to worry about it right now."

"You do if you ever want to go on a second date. The death glare you gave Fiona's dessert could have made it burst into flames."

"The baked Alaska was already on fire." Liam grinned. Her teasing him about his diet was the most personal they had been in weeks.

Deidre pulled the ponytail band out of her hair and looped it around her wrist. Bending forward, she separated her braid into a riot of waves. Usually, she had her hair up or hidden. It always caught him off guard how long it was. Liam reached out to touch a strand, realizing he should pull his hand back just as she whipped her head up. Hair wrapped around his wrist and caught in his watch, stopping her progress.

"Ouch!" Deidre's hand followed the entangled hair as she frantically tried to release it. Their fingers touched and she froze. "Is that your watch?"

"Yes."

She felt along his arm to his hand and back. "Can you take your watch off?"

Liam unbuckled the latch, and her hair fell free. "Sorry about that. I didn't realize ..."

Deidre rubbed her head. "I guess I should have warned you. My hair is like Velcro. It grabs everything."

"It doesn't feel like Velcro." Liam reached for a lock and rubbed the fine strands between his thumb and fingers. "Unless you mean the soft side."

Her brown eyes were close enough he could see a golden ring around them. They had more depth than he'd assumed, drawing him closer.

Deidre's hand on his chest stopped him. "Boss, I think whatever idea is going through your head right now is as bad as dissing my muffins." She gave him a gentle shove.

"Sorry. I don't know—"

Deidre stood. "I think they call it stir crazy. Perhaps you've discovered the true secret to why women bear the offspring. Men don't have enough patience to get through a pregnancy."

"A generalization?" Liam smiled so she would know he was teasing. "However, in this case, I'd call it spot on. How are you not going crazy?"

"Abbie's movie marathons. I voted for Colin Firth with a side note that the Bollywood version had the catchiest music. And then I've been catching up on my TBR pile."

"TBR?"

"To be read. The dozens of books I have been downloading and never gotten to, and then there is knitting hats."

"Knitting?" I've never seen you knit." Liam followed Deidre out of the gazebo.

"Recent hobby. Abbie bought these circular looms so we could knit hats for the homeless while we watch TV. It's relaxing. You need to go do something you enjoy."

"As soon as this assignment is done, I want to go rock climbing. I've missed that."

"There is an indoor wall near here. You should go."

"Come with me?" Rock climbing was one of the ultimate trust exercises, having to depend on each other to belay the lines.

Deidre shook her head. "Last time we both left at the same time, Abbie had false labor. We've made it to June 13, the first day of the safe range. I don't want to tempt Murphy's law. Another week would be ideal."

"You don't want to climb with me."

"I don't really want to climb with anyone. Been there, done that."

Liam held the door to the employee entrance open for her. "Sounds like you didn't go with the right person if you feel that way."

"Probably not." Deidre stopped in front of her bedroom door. "You should go today. According to the doctor this morning, today shouldn't be a baby birthday."

"Oh, the puns." Liam slapped his palm to his forehead. "If you are all right with it, I will go."

Deidre gave him a smile, which made him wish she hadn't stopped the potential kiss, even if she was right to keep things professional.

Two hours later, Liam was racing to the top of a fabricated cliff. Alone.

Abbie waved Deidre over to a seat in the theater room. "You're just in time. I found a *Sense and Sensibility* version spelled S-c-e-n-t-s. It's a modern remake. Do you have time to watch?"

"Technically, it's my siesta time, so I can watch the whole thing with you." Deidre sat down in a leather recliner.

"My mom is around here someplace. She says lying around watching TV all day is driving her crazy." Abbie started the video. A few minutes in, Abbie gasped.

Deidre looked from the screen, where very little had happened, to Abbie. "What? The plot isn't hard to figure out."

"I think—" Abbie pushed out of her recliner. "I think my water broke!"

Deidre jumped out of her chair and turned up the lights. "I think you may be right. Contractions?"

"Some pain through my back."

Deidre pulled out her phone. "Get your mom in here. Is Preston home?"

"I sent him to the office after the appointment. I get tired of him sitting and staring at me."

"Call him after your mom. I'm alerting the detail."

Mrs. Hastings took one look at Abbie and called the doctor.

Thirty minutes later, Deidre stood outside the intake room at the hospital.

Liam rushed up the hallway. "What's the situation?"

"Abbie's water broke, so she is here until the delivery. They won't stop the contractions now. They aren't very strong yet, but labor can change fast. Only family and one nurse are inside."

"So this is no false alarm, then. Did you get your siesta?"

"Only the first ten minutes."

"The motor home will be here in ten if you want to try to get some rest now."

"It is tempting, but I don't think I could sleep."

Dr. Song came out. "The family has authorized me to tell you we are moving Mrs. Harmon to the larger of the maternity operating rooms. Given the situation, I'm more comfortable with not moving her later if we need to. Ms. Ross, you will need to be in a sterile gown or set of scrubs, which the hospital can loan you. We are proceeding with Mrs. Harmon's plan for a natural birth. I won't require you to wear a mask unless we do an emergency surgery."

"Will anyone be wearing masks?" Almost anyone could get past them in a surgeon's mask.

"Not unless we do the surgery."

As the hours dragged on past midnight, Abbie asked to walk around the hallways. The doctor granted permission. Deidre relayed the request.

"Absolutely not." Liam's voice came over the earpiece loud and clear.

"Not your call." When he was in labor, he could bark orders.

"We can't bring in any more of the detail, and I think all 180 babies for the day are trying to be born here tonight."

"The surgery hall is contained and locked. It isn't busy at your end, is it?"

Liam took a moment to answer. "Not as much as the main floor, but everyone is in scrubs, and a few people are in masks. I don't like it."

"Jethro Hastings is in the waiting room, right?"

"Yes."

"Any of the brothers?"

"I see where you are going with this. Do you think they will let them in?"

Deidre stepped farther into the corner. "I'll get Mrs. Hastings to ask. They may let someone in."

"I'll go fill them in. I have an extra earpiece."

Deidre waited until Mrs. Hastings had helped Abbie into a robe. "We are concerned about the number of people on the floor. Can you request Jethro and a son join us for the walk?"

"That's a wonderful idea." Mrs. Hastings crossed the room and spoke with the nurse. The nurse spoke into the in-house radio that hung around her neck. Deidre tried to follow the quiet conversation. Mrs. Hastings held up one finger and signed the letter *J*.

Deidre tapped her earpiece. "Jethro can come back."

"The nurse just came out for him."

Abbie took a few awkward steps, then stopped to lean on her husband. When the contraction passed, she shuffled out the door and into the hallway. Jethro and Liam stood on the other side of the secure doors.

The nurse directed them out of the surgery hall. "We can't block this hallway. I'm sorry."

Deidre repeated the instructions. "Liam, take forward. Jethro, stay with the principal. I'll take rear."

Jethro laughed into his comm. "Like you could give me any other position."

"I would not have dreamed of it. Is there anything I need to know?" Deidre stretched her neck, reminding herself that Abbie was more tired.

Alan's voice came over the comms. "Hospital security came around the waiting room, checking ID. They asked three people to leave."

That meant hospital security was working with them. "Sorry to have to leave you out there, Alan."

"I'd rather be out here than in there. I'm ready to be an uncle, not witness the process."

Abbie stopped and leaned on Preston again. Deidre checked her watch. Four minutes apart. Poor Abbie looked as if she'd spent two hours in the gym going a round with each of her brothers. A nurse directed them into the main floor so they wouldn't block the surgical hall. They slowed to a turtle's pace as Abbie continued walking down the hall. Liam was right. The floor was more crowded than they had planned on. Deidre wondered if it was the proverbial full moon, but she had no way to check and hadn't been paying attention to a lunar calendar.

Twenty minutes later, Abbie signaled she was ready to go back to the room. The nurse stopped Jethro and Liam at the entrance of the surgery wing. "You two can't go in, sorry."

Confident there was no one behind her, Deidre hurried into the surgery room. A new nurse was there, one Deidre had met the other day. Everyone else came in. Abbie stopped to breathe through another contraction. Still about four minutes apart.

Liam's voice came over the comms. "I am going to take a break. One of Preston's detail is spelling me off. Do you need anything?"

"I could use ten minutes and a restroom. This room is secure."

"I'll watch from here."

"Thanks, boss."

Guilt for not being able to help Deidre more made even a twenty-minute nap impossible. Liam had lain on the motor home's couch bed, staring at the plastic ceiling for two hours. Liam checked his watch. Seven o'clock. Deidre had been up for twenty-six hours now. The last report indicated labor was still progressing. Whatever that meant. He tapped his earpiece. "Deidre, how are you doing?"

"Well enough. I'd like another ten-minute break, but I'd rather you be in the hallway. The nurses changed shifts an hour ago, and I want someone familiar with faces.

"I'll be up in ten. Do you need anything?"

"A protein bar would be great. I'll even take one of those keto things of yours."

Liam chuckled. "Anything else?"

"No, thanks."

Liam put on a new shirt and checked with the rest of the detail. They'd put guards in the main-floor public lobbies, rotating them every four hours. They weren't so much watching as they were close by to respond. Preston Harmon's parents were landing at the airport in an hour. Another set of bodyguards to deal with. Jethro and the Hasting brothers had been rotating in and out all night, passing the earpiece back and forth and giving the detail any news about the labor-and-delivery waiting room.

Liam notified Deidre as soon as he got off the elevator.

She met him in the hallway outside the surgery doors. She seemed alert and exhausted all at once. She would crash when the adrenaline from this job wore off. Liam made a mental note to make sure she had a ride after the delivery.

"Abbie requested her father join her. Mrs. Hastings told me to take thirty minutes. I have permission to use the couch in the staff lounge. Wish me luck on a power nap. FYI, Jethro is definitely watching the room more than he is Abbie." She gave him a half smile. Liam assumed there was a joke there, though he didn't quite understand since everything he knew about labor and delivery came from television.

Liam handed her the protein bar—Deidre's brand, not his. "Anything else I can get for you?"

"Make a note to have two female bodyguards next time this happens."

"Mrs. Harmon only mentioned the need for one."

"That's because her last official job was in the delivery room with Mandy Crawford the night Joy was born. And the delivery took less than three hours." Deidre checked her watch. "I'll be back in twenty-six minutes."

Liam watched her enter an employee-only door. An extra female would have been good. With Mia off painkillers, she could have helped to some extent. Or even one of the trained nannies. So much for his well-thought-out plan.

THE POWER NAP HELPED MORE than Deidre could have thought possible. When she returned to the surgery unit, little had changed. Abbie lay facedown on a giant beanbag, working through a contraction, Preston rubbing her back.

Jethro wasted no time leaving the room. "It's too hard for me to watch."

"Thanks for the break."

Deidre took up her post, ignoring Abbie as much as she could to stay focused on the others in the room.

Lunchtime came and went. Mrs. Hastings and Preston took turns leaving for a bite to eat. Deidre grabbed a ten-minute break.

The doctor, in a new set of scrubs, checked Abbie's progress and turned to the nurse. "Call for the teams. We will see baby number one very soon."

"They are calling in the neonatal teams." Deidre relayed the information. They expected nine to twelve extra people in the room. The doors opened, admitting the first team—a doctor and two nurses, all whom Abbie recognized. Two other teams followed in quick succession. All three teams went through equipment that had been sitting idle since yesterday. Incubators, heat lamps, monitors, and drawers of tubes and tools were all double-checked.

One of Dr. Song's partners entered with an anesthesiologist and another assistant. Deidre checked the hospital employee list to verify the assistant, who hadn't been cleared before. From the conversation between the assistant and the anesthesiologist, it was clear they'd worked together often. Trusting her instincts, Deidre nodded the unexpected employee in before hospital security sent her the verification.

Abbie moaned the loudest she had thus far. Activity around her bed increased, and one of the neonatal teams stood ready, focused solely on Dr. Song.

"Good job. Once more." The doctor's voice carried over the others'.

A wail. Someone called out the time: 13:14. Military time, of course.

One of the assistants on the second team held up his tablet as he took down patient information. No, he had an iPad. The hospital didn't use iPads to track patient information— they used another brand.

"Contact security." Deidre said the words and moved between Abbie and the assistant, snatching the iPad out of his hands. "Sir, this equipment is not authorized. Come with me."

The man tried to push Deidre out of the way. A reflection at the corner of his glasses caught the light. Video. She dropped the iPad. Alan could figure out what was on it even if the screen shattered. The man bent down to retrieve it. Not wanting to cause too much of a disturbance, Deidre grabbed his hand in a hold guaranteed to get his attention—and cooperation. "Please join me in the hallway." She propelled him out of the room.

Two hospital security guards waited outside the operating room. Deidre spoke, knowing her comms would pick up the conversation. "This man had an iPad and was taking photos. I believe there's a camera in his glasses as well. Dermot Security would like to review the electronics, please." She handed the employee over.

"Where's the iPad?" asked one of the hospital guards while the other put the man in handcuffs.

"I'll get it. You should take off his glasses." Deidre checked through the window before reentering the surgery. She could see the doctor from the first neonatal team carrying the baby over to Preston. Was it alive? They hadn't connected any wires or tubes to it. Deidre stood frozen in the vestibule, her heart stopped.

"Deidre?" Liam's voice came over the comms, propelling her into action. She needed the iPad. As she pushed open the door, the thin wail of a baby filled the room. Deidre's heart rate returned to normal as she scooped the iPad off the floor and rushed it out to the waiting guard. "It doesn't look broken."

The guard nodded.

Before returning to the operating room, Deidre stopped to wash her hands up to the elbows, then watched through the window. Mrs. Hastings now held her grandson as Preston moved back to Abbie's side.

"Deidre?" Liam's voice again.

"Yes."

"Are you all right? It looked like you froze."

"I was just checking the room before I reentered." Close enough to the truth. "Order a sweep of the room and the equipment. He may have placed a microcamera somewhere before I caught him. I'm sure he's one of the cleared employees."

"He is. Or was. I am sure his new status is 'former employee.'"

Mrs. Hastings came over with her bundle of joy. "Can you believe it? Five pounds, four ounces, and an Apgar of nine. Now, what was that scuffle?"

"Taken care of. Sorry you had to notice."

"I don't think Abbie did."

Good to know.

"Abbie wants to see Brandon again," called Preston, saving Deidre from answering or being too close to the newborn.

Deidre gave the second incubator—where the man had spent most of his time—a quick once-over. A black button seemed out of place. There wasn't one on the third NICU bed. The nurse closest to the second incubator watched Abbie with narrowed eyes. Deidre pointed to the black camera. "Excuse me, is this button a normal part of the bed?"

The nurse's eyes widened. "No! Doctor!"

The second-team doctor turned. "What?"

The nurse pointed to the camera. "Our equipment has been tampered with."

The doctor turned to the third team. "You're up next." He pushed a button on the communication radio hanging around his neck. "I need a new NICU bed, stat. Someone's compromised this one."

Abbie groaned again. Mrs. Hastings passed the baby she held to the nurse from the first team as the doctor encouraged Abbie. Deidre did her best to ignore the activity, instead scanning the room for any more cameras. She tapped her comms. "Liam, I found a camera on the NICU bed. Can someone question that guy? The doctor refuses to use the bed. I don't want anything else compromised."

"I'll inform security."

"Thanks."

Another baby's wail enlisted cheers from everyone near the bed.

"13:37."

The third team sprang into action. An orderly tapped on the door, and the second doctor nodded to Deidre. "You can let him in with the bed. I recognize him."

Deidre opened the door. Once the doctor had inspected the new bed, the orderly left.

A grunt worthy of a finals round of a black-belt sparring came from Abbie.

"13:49." A third cry joined the jubilation. Tears streamed down Abbie's face and disappeared in her smile.

Someone gave Abbie the first baby to hold while Preston held the second. The third remained with the neonatal team.

"Five."

No, not a low Apgar. Deidre couldn't pull her eyes away. *Please, no. Please, no*. The prayer came unbidden. The doctor worked on the baby, his back to her. The nurses kept their bodies between the baby and the new parents.

The room grew silent as the neonatal team continued their work.

Please, no. Please, no. Deidre watched with the others.

Mrs. Hastings came over with the baby she held and spoke to the doctor in a hushed tone. The doctor nodded and took the baby Mrs. Hastings held and unwrapped him, laying him next to his brother.

A nurse smiled. Mrs. Hastings signaled Preston to bring the child he held. The doctor laid the baby on the other side of their little brother as the team continued to work.

"Seven, no, eight. Mark Apgar as eight."

The neonatal teams exchanged hopeful glances. Preston pulled out his phone and took a photo—one destined to go viral with the tag line "We are our brother's keeper."

Thank you. Thank you. Deidre sent the thought up before the next thought could assail her. Why hadn't she had a miracle like that?

A nurse requested that the Hastings and Harmon families come into the small consulting room, the guards from the older Mr. Harmon's detail excluded. Judging from the cheer, the babies had arrived safely. Why hadn't Deidre come out yet?

"Deidre, status?"

"Finishing up. I'll come out when they move her to a room. Not sure where they will move the boys."

"Are they well?"

There was a long pause. "Better than expected."

"That doesn't tell me anything."

"HIPAA."

He could almost imagine her smiling as she said it. Even if she was correct, he would find out when the family told him. "Mia is tired of desk duty. After being up here, I think she could watch the nursery if the boys need to be in there."

"That should work." The exhaustion in Deidre's voice was evident, even through the earpiece. Liam checked the time. Not counting whatever relief she had from the brief power nap, Deidre had been awake for over thirty-four hours. And removed a threat. The photos from the iPad, video glasses, and button camera were in police custody, as was the former neonatal nurse. The hospital was pressing HIPAA-related charges. The Harmons' lawyers were hoping for something more as well as getting whatever footage or stills had been taken back from the police before they could be leaked. The hospital security guards let Alan, the Hastings Security IT guru, examine the confiscated equipment while they waited for the police. He was confident none of the data had been transferred outside the hospital.

Preston Harmon came out of the surgery wing and into the small room where the family was. Liam told the other Harmon guard to watch the room while he remained at the end of the hallway leading to the operating rooms. Nodding and smiling at Liam, the nurses wheeled an empty NICU bed out.

Preston came back up the hallway holding his phone. "You need to see this."

Liam took the phone. The three babies lay side by side, the two on the outside each with an arm wrapped around the one in the center, their little legs all tangled together like some sea creature.

"Each of them is over five pounds. The doctor can't believe it. Davis had a little trouble at first, but when we put Brandon and Connor with him, he perked right up. Melanie's idea. They will keep the boys in the nursery for a couple hours, mostly to watch Davis."

Liam handed the phone back. "The employee who was taking the photos is in the custody of the police. No photos were transmitted."

"Photos? Employee? What are you talking about?" Preston didn't put his phone away.

He hadn't noticed. It was exactly what Deidre had hoped for—not upset the principals if there was a problem. "Ms. Ross caught one of the neonatal nurses trying to take photos. We think he got in because all the doctors thought he was on someone else's team. Ms. Ross removed him quickly."

"She must have because I didn't even notice. Glad you took care of it. Abbie was spectacular. The doctors thought they'd have to do a C-section, but everything worked out. It's rare to deliver three naturally. My wife is amazing. Here she is, holding Brandon." Preston held up his phone again. "Fatherhood, wow. You need to be a father. It's amazing. I need to show my mom this." Preston rushed into the waiting room.

Liam waited for Deidre, ignoring his longing for tea parties with his own wife and children.

THE ROOM TRANSFER WAS ACCOMPLISHED with little fuss. Abbie wanted the boys with her, and the doctor agreed to it after monitoring the smallest boy, though he insisted a nurse remain in the room. Deidre followed the entourage out, knowing Liam was keeping watch somewhere ahead of the group.

Deidre wished she had pockets, her hands were shaking so bad. She needed to get out of the hospital now. With the three baby boys safe in the arms of Abbie, Preston, and Mrs. Hastings, and three of the four Hastings brothers sitting in the waiting room, plus Preston's detail, the maternity floor was currently the safest place on the planet. As the last of the nurses left the room, Jethro nodded at Deidre, signaling that she could leave too.

As soon as she stepped outside the door, she tapped her comms piece. "Family has requested alone time. External guard only. I am on break." There was no point in giving her name. If Liam's people didn't know after the last thirty-five hours that hers was the only female voice on comms, they had a bigger problem to deal with. She pulled out the earpiece to give her ear a rest and headed to the visitor locker room to change out of the scrubs. Thankfully, yesterday's clothes hadn't picked up the smells of the hospital. Images she'd suppressed but had never forgotten plagued her.

The fewer reminders the better. Now, to exit the hospital before the emotions brewing inside her came to the surface.

Fifty feet to the elevator, forty, thirty. Adam Hastings waved and grinned a big goofy smile, his girlfriend September at his side.

Twenty.

Ten.

Deidre pushed the elevator call button and tried a deep-breathing technique. She only had to hold it together until she got to her car.

Ping.

The up arrow glowed green above the elevator.

Deidre took another cleansing breath and checked the call button to make sure the light was still lit.

Ping.

The red down arrow glowed over the other elevator. The doors slid open, revealing an empty elevator. Deidre stepped inside and pressed the button for the lobby. As the doors closed, she slumped against the wall.

"Wait!" An arm shot through the opening, forcing the elevator doors open. Liam. "Didn't you hear me?"

It took too much effort to respond. Deidre opened her hand and held out her earpiece to him. He took it. He was wearing a different shirt. Had he been able to change and shower? A shower sounded heavenly.

"I'm driving you."

No. She needed to be alone. She shook her head.

Liam placed his hands on her shoulders. "Deidre, you are dead on your feet. I am driving you either to your apartment or the mansion, where you will take a full twenty-four-hour break. We have Mrs. Harmon and the babies covered. Mrs. Hastings says she isn't leaving."

"She is tired too. And poor Abbie. I'll come back after a break. Twenty-four off is too long." She actually did need to leave and stay away, but admitting her weakness to Liam wasn't an option.

Had her words been coherent?

The elevator slowed to a stop. Deidre tried to duck around Liam, but her reflexes were slow, and she had to put a hand against the elevator wall to steady herself. He let her out of the elevator and walked by her side. If he chose right now as his anytime, anywhere showdown, she'd lose. She didn't have the strength to tackle a ten-year-old. But she could drive home.

"My car or yours?"

Deidre kept walking to the section of the lot she'd parked in yesterday, her legs on autopilot. She pulled the keys out of her pocket and hit the key fob to unlock the door, only to find her thumb connecting with her empty palm.

Liam held up the keys. "You are not driving. I should have never been able to get those away from you."

"I don't want to drive. I just want to be alone." The tears she'd dammed up for the last three and a half hours broke free and rushed down her face. Liam's countenance blurred. *Stupid man! Why can't he go away?*

Strong arms encircled her.

Deidre did the last thing she wanted to do, crumbling in his arms as her tears fell freely. She needed this so much.

Surprised by Deidre's reaction, Liam did the only thing he could do. He held her. A few passersby looked twice and gave him sympathetic looks. In a hospital parking lot, no explanations were needed.

When Deidre pulled back and began searching her pockets, Liam wished he carried a handkerchief like his father used to. She found a wrinkled tissue and wiped her face. "I'm sorry. I shouldn't—" She hiccupped.

"It's been a long day and a half. Let me drive you home." Liam unlocked the car and held open the passenger door.

Deidre wilted into the car. Liam double-checked to make sure she was completely in before shutting the door and hurrying around to the driver's side. He opened the door and spoke before she could. Obviously, he didn't want to hear an apology or excuse. "Your apartment or the mansion?"

"There's a hotel a block over. I was going to check in there."

Liam started the car and cranked up the AC. "Why?"

"That way, I'm close if I'm needed. I don't think I can sleep in the motor home with the rest of the detail coming in and out. I have my go-bag."

"We got this covered. Go sleep in a familiar bed. Not some bed three hundred people and whatever germs they carried have slept in already this year."

"Gross."

"Exactly. Now, which do you want—the mansion or your apartment?"

There was a long pause. "Just take me to the hotel."

"Deidre, I need you at your best when your next shift begins. Where do you want to go? And don't say hotel. No one sleeps well in a hotel."

She looked at the ceiling of the car and took a deep breath. It may have been a prayer for patience. "Right now, I'll sleep better in the hotel. The mansion is too far away, and there are too many memories in my condo to let me sleep."

Memories? "Do you need to talk about today? Decompress? That might let you sleep."

"No. I just need to go to the hotel. Please." A pleading, almost whimper entered her voice. New tears glistened at the corners of her eyes.

He didn't like her choice, but it wasn't worth the argument. If Mia could take a shift at night when the boys were likely to be in the nursery, Deidre wouldn't be needed at all. "Fine, I'll take you to the hotel. Will you tell me what happened?"

Deidre shot him a look and quickly turned away. "Nothing

happened. I'm just tired."

"Liar." A car pulled out behind them, so Liam stayed in the parking space.

"What do you want me to say? You don't really want to hear about my daughter, who only lived six hours, or how I didn't know she died because I was in ICU. Or how my husband came home three months later and asked for a divorce since there was a 30 percent chance that if I tried to have another child, the complications could result in the same outcome and he wanted to be a dad. Oh, and his girlfriend was six months pregnant." Deidre's voice rose as she talked. She yanked on the door handle and pushed open her door, but her seat belt held her in place. She fumbled with the latch.

Liam grabbed both of her hands in his. "I want to listen if you'll tell me. Because if what I am picturing is true, then witnessing the births of three children with doctors rushing around must have been difficult beyond anything I've ever done."

A new stream of tears ran from Deidre's eyes.

Liam lifted one hand to her cheek and wiped away the tears with his thumb. "Do you know how brave and strong and amazing that makes you?"

Deidre shook her head. "But I'm not."

Someone passed by, bumping Deidre's door most of the way closed. Liam brought his other hand to her face. How could he get her to see herself as he saw her? He didn't even think as he lowered his head and touched his lips to hers. And she didn't pull back or do any number of the things she could have to stop him. He angled his head and moved his hands into her hair to hold her in place as she responded to his kiss. Her ex-husband was an idiot for giving up a woman who kissed like this—a woman who was all strength, beauty, and brains. Liam deepened the kiss, obliterating all thoughts of her faceless ex in his mind and hopefully hers. He pulled back.

Deidre turned away.

No! His heart raced as if all the security alarms had been tripped at once.

Deidre closed the car door and turned back to face him. "The AC is running." She gave him the smallest of smiles and shrugged a shoulder.

Liam searched for something to say. "Whoever he was, he was an idiot. I've wanted to kiss you since the first time we hugged in the gym. You are the most amazing, talented, and beautiful woman I've ever met." He traced a single finger along her jawline.

Deidre took the gesture as an invitation and leaned in to kiss him again. Liam didn't stop her. Although as exhausted as he was and she must be, he was careful not to go further than gentle kisses. There would be no regrets later.

Making out like a teenager would have been a good way to describe the next five minutes of Deidre's life. They finally ended the kiss when someone in the parking lot catcalled. Deidre settled back into her seat as Liam pulled out of the parking space, a host of emotions battling for prominence in her. Despair and euphoria took center stage. Had they both been less exhausted, the kiss might not have happened, and that would be a shame. Yes, she'd wanted to kiss him and wouldn't mind more. Something in the contact had healed a tiny corner of her soul. For the first time in what felt like forever, she felt desired. And Liam hadn't taken advantage of her emotional state and pushed for more than she was offering, his hands never dropping below her shoulders. He had to be almost as tired as she was. Only the endorphins of the kiss kept her running.

"I still don't know where to take you." Liam interrupted her thoughts.

"The condo was part of my divorce settlement. I don't want to be there now. I know the mansion will be quiet, but it's so far away—"

Liam took a left out of the parking lot. "I have an idea, and I am not trying to push our kisses further or anything. My apartment isn't too far from here. You can sleep there. I won't even come inside." A thin line of pink flushed above his collar.

Deidre turned the idea over. If anyone found out, there would be some explaining to do.

"I'll take an Uber back to the hospital so you are free to leave when you wish. Text me when you leave."

She checked her watch. "When does your shift end?"

"Never."

"That isn't what I meant."

He glanced at the clock on the dash. "Three hours, more or less."

"I'll leave before then."

"No need. I can go back to the mansion. I'm not putting you back in the rotation for at least twenty-four hours." Liam pulled into his parking garage and into a numbered spot. "Don't worry, this is my spot. As long as I don't complain, you won't be towed."

Deidre got out and held out her hand to Liam. He handed over her keys. As she opened the trunk and went to grab her duffel, Liam reached around her and grabbed it first. "Allow me."

At the elevator, he punched in a code, not bothering to hide the numbers from Deidre. She couldn't help memorizing the pattern.

"You caught those, right?"

"Sorry, yes."

Liam laughed. "Don't be sorry. I want you to have them. You might need them. That's my code. Each resident has a different one."

The door slid open. As the elevator ascended, any remaining energy Deidre had was left below. The exhilaration of the kisses had worn off, supplanted by fatigue and confusion. If she hadn't been so tired, she would never have allowed or invited… That was a lie. Her heart knew what her mind wasn't allowing.

The elevator bumped to a halt. Deidre followed Liam down the hall to a door he opened using the same code. He set the duffel inside, then held the door open for her. "There are some meals in the freezer. I haven't been here for days, so don't trust the milk."

The place was clean and neat—exactly what she would have expected from someone so recently in the military.

"There are extra towels under the left-hand counter in the bathroom. And the control to the AC is—"

Deidre held up her hand. "Just come in and show me."

He stood in the doorway for a moment before crossing the room to the thermostat. "The AC is set on eighty-seven while I am away. Is seventy-two okay?"

Deidre nodded, and he pushed the numbers to change it. She followed him into the bedroom, where the bed was made with military precision. In the bathroom, he pulled out a set of blue towels and placed them on the end of the counter. Deidre gave him plenty of space to leave the room. Liam stopped in the kitchen and opened the fridge. "Definitely do not drink the milk. Do you want me to bring you anything?"

"I'll be fine." She leaned one arm on the counter to support herself.

"Then I'll get back to the hospital. Sleep well." He kissed her cheek. Opening the door, he looked back. "I would have given you a better kiss goodbye, but you're too tired and I'm too ... too ... interested."

The door shut, Liam locking it from the outside with the keypad—or so she assumed from the beeps.

Interested? What an interesting word to use. Wow, her comprehension had disintegrated. She used the wall to support herself on her walk down the hall, then stepped out of her shoes and collapsed on top of his bed. Sleep overcame her before she could ponder what he'd meant.

As expected, the rest of the afternoon was quiet. Liam supervised the coordination of the various security teams and Hastings family in a way that wouldn't make the other new mothers nervous. During a shift change, he counted fifteen bodyguards on the floor, more than the president of the United States needed at a state dinner in a hostile country. The floor supervisor frowned at him. At least she only saw nine. His count included Abbie's brothers and parents. He called Mia into work.

Still wearing a wrist brace, she wasn't ready for full duty, but she was the least conspicuous when it came to monitoring the nursery the boys had been moved to. Liam moved the rest of the teams down to the main level. Most of the hospital staff was tolerant of the disruption. After catching their own employee working with the paparazzi, the hospital director eased up on the number of bodyguards allowed as long as they stayed out of everyone's way. The gift baskets and food Preston Harmon had provided for each employee who worked the floor, from custodian to doctor, hadn't hurt. And the box-seat tickets to upcoming games at Wrigley Field had been staggered over several dates so the nursing schedules could accommodate everyone having a turn.

Liam walked through all the security stations one last time before turning the next shift over to his father. "Everything is quiet. I'm assuming word got out about the unfortunate paparazzi. Preston has agreed to do a smile and wave as they leave the hospital. His mother will hold one baby, Melanie Hastings another, and Abbie the third. The grandfathers and Preston will accompany them. The Hastings brothers will not be in uniform, but they will be present. Four bodyguards should be more than enough. The Harmon's PR manager wants something longer."

Simon looked over the plan on Liam's tablet. "So, we know about timing yet?"

"Not yet. The smallest boy was having problems maintaining his temperature. I've heard Sunday mentioned a few times."

Simon frowned. "Slow news day will have everyone and their intern here. However, the drive back to the estate will be clearer."

"I'd like two in the morning, but I doubt our new mom will."

"That would be a nice time. Too bad none of our clients ever wants to travel in the middle of the night." Simon gave Liam one of his dad looks. "You look tired. Those two four-hour breaks you took weren't enough."

"More than we could give Deidre."

Simon nodded. "I saw she was on for thirty-six hours. Whatever she was supposed to make, double it and offer to pay Hastings enough that she can have an extra week of paid vacation."

"That's a good idea. Maybe I'll take one too."

"It won't be paid." Simon laughed. "You're salaried. Go get some rest. I'll text you when I know the schedule."

Liam checked his phone app for his apartment security. He didn't want to invade Deidre's privacy, but he needed to know when he could safely go back, so he activated only the motion detector by the front door.

No activity.

He drove past the bakery. According to the sign, it was nearly closing time. Maybe they still had some of those cranberry muffins. He could sneak in and leave them on the table for Deidre. Liam circled the block. Luck was on his side. They had three left. On his way to the apartment, he stopped at the store and bought a half gallon of milk. Before entering his apartment, he checked the app again. Still no movement. His plan was simple: in, bag on the table, milk in the fridge, out. Forty-five seconds max.

The front door opened soundlessly. The kitchen was empty. Without turning on the light, he deposited the muffins on the table and put the milk away. Liam opened the corner drawer to look for a pen to leave a note so Deidre would know the muffins were for her. As he closed the drawer and turned around, his feet suddenly left the floor and he was on his back. A shadowy figure stood over him.

"Liam?"

What had she done? Deidre felt along the wall above the counter for a light. A groan came from the floor. Her fingers found the edge of a plastic rectangle, and she flipped the switch. A high-pitched grinding noise filled the room. Deidre turned off the disposal and flipped the other switch, the light above the sink illuminating the disaster she'd caused.

Liam sat on the floor holding his head.

Deidre knelt next to him. "I am so sorry. You said you weren't coming back, and when I saw someone looking for a knife in the dark, I reacted." She offered him a hand up.

"A knife? I was looking for a pen."

"You don't keep knives in that drawer?"

Liam half shook his head and groaned.

"You need ice." She grabbed a towel off a peg and scooped some ice out of the freezer bin. "Sit down. This will help."

Taking the ice from her, he lowered himself into a chair. "Is this what you meant by anytime, anyplace?"

Deidre pulled out another chair. "Not exactly. I meant in a sparring match. I didn't mean to hurt you. I just—"

"Did the same thing I would have done if I'd found someone scrounging through the kitchen drawers in the dark. Only I might have turned the light on first."

"I couldn't find the switch."

"I noticed."

"I'm so sorry. I really am."

Liam held up a hand. "I'm good." He removed the ice pack. "If I hadn't already revised and recanted my opinion of female bodyguards, your move would have convinced me. Why didn't you use that move on me in the gym?"

Deidre shrugged. "I guess you were never in the right position for me to try it."

Liam held up the bakery bag. "I brought you muffins."

"Now I feel really bad. You were trying to do something nice for me, and I repaid you by flooring you."

"Show me how to do that move, and we'll be even. I didn't think anyone could put me on the floor so fast, even if I wasn't expecting it."

The move was the one Abbie had designed, but Deidre had added her own twist to it. "I can, but the move only works against a larger mass. All the Hastings brothers have tried it. In an even match, it's useless."

"Well, I might go up against Goliath one day." His smile didn't reach his pain-filled eyes.

Deidre pushed back her chair. "I think I am fine to go back to the estate now."

Liam put a hand on her arm. "You don't need to rush off. You've only had, what, five hours of sleep?"

"I can drive for twenty minutes. Then you can get some rest in your own home. When is my next shift?"

"There isn't one. The babies are here. Dad told me to tell you job well done and pay Hastings whatever it takes to get you a week of paid vacation plus a bonus."

"I guess I fulfilled my contract. I hadn't realized the job would end so soon." Jobs always ended. Why did she feel such a sense of loss at the idea that this one was over?

"I know Mrs. Harmon is still in the hospital, but you aren't ready to go back on a shift yet." Liam rubbed the back of his head. "Mostly. You need to be alert. Mia has a wrist brace on, but she can finish the hospital shift if needed. Mrs. Hastings will take care of anything more personal on Abbie's end. To be honest, the Hastings brothers are in our way. I've had to move most of our guards off the floor."

"I can only imagine. The poor nurses. Even with Preston's gifts, it must be stressful for them."

He pushed the bakery bag over. "Eat a muffin."

"Bossy much?"

Liam looked at his watch. "Technically, you still work for me, so, yeah, I'll be bossy."

"Three? You better eat at least one." Deidre placed a muffin in front of him.

He broke the muffin in half. "A few carbs might not kill me. Do you want any milk?"

"Fresh?"

"Not farm fresh but as good as I can buy in town."

"Yes, please."

Liam dumped the ice in the sink before pouring them both a glass. "So, what will you do with your vacation time?"

"Other than sleep? I don't know. I haven't been to Mackinac Island in a while, and there is a living-history museum, more of a town, on the Mississippi. I could repaint the condo." The chit-chat didn't answer any of the questions she hoped it would. Now that she was fully awake, the fact that they were eating muffins and milk and discussing nothing of consequence seemed out of place. She'd dropped her deepest secret on him, and he'd kissed her.

A lot.

Maybe it was a guy thing. Maybe he didn't care. She finished her muffin and rinsed her glass. "Thanks for letting me crash here." Before he could react, she gathered her keys and phone from his bedroom. She smoothed the wrinkles on the bedspread until every trace of her was gone.

Liam leaned against the bedroom doorjamb, arms crossed. "You don't need to rush off. I was going to go back to the estate."

"It's better if I go. This is your place. I need to pack up there anyway."

He moved back but not enough to let her by. "You know we need to talk, right? A conversation for when we're both fully awake."

"About?"

"What happened in the parking lot and what you said."

"There isn't much to say."

"I think there is. But not now, and definitely not in my bedroom."

"Later then?" *More like never.* Talking about the kiss was one thing. They could both pass it off as being too tired and too emotional and part as friends. But she wasn't ready to share beyond what she had said about her past. Not that there was much more to the story anyway.

Liam stepped back, and Deidre slipped past him. He followed her to the door, where he stopped her with a touch on her arm. "I'm serious about the talk." He brushed a kiss across her cheek. If she turned toward him, it could become more. Deidre left before giving in to temptation.

Liam felt around for his phone only to realize he was in his apartment and the noise really was his alarm clock. He absently wondered if it went off every day. Sitting up, he checked the messages on his phone. The doctors wanted to keep Mrs. Harmon and the boys another twenty-four hours. His father had planned a hospital rotation schedule that didn't include him or Deidre. The press conference was tentatively scheduled for eleven o'clock the next morning, late enough to miss any Sunday-morning talk shows. Deidre hadn't checked in, but her locater in the security app showed she was at the estate.

After his shower, Liam stood in front of his closet. Most of his clothes had migrated to the estate in the last month. His choices were one of the many logo T-shirts or a pink polo an ex-girlfriend had given him one Christmas. He wasn't sure why he'd kept it. He chose a shirt advertising a 5k he'd participated in last time he'd been home on leave.

The guards at the estate gate stopped him long enough to ask if he'd seen the newest Harmons and how the family was doing. No one was in the employee common area. Liam passed Deidre's partially opened door and paused. She never left her door open. A polka-dotted carry-on sat next to the doorframe.

Perhaps she was loading her car. He tapped on the door. "Deidre?"

No answer.

Liam crossed the hall to the room he had used. The laundry service had cleaned all his shirts and one of his suits. He would miss that perk on whatever assignment his father put him on next. Laundry and the swim spa. Already he'd added the spa to his bucket list of things to buy. His father hadn't taken him up on the idea of getting one for the firm.

Liam carried his shirts, still on hangers, to his car. The suitcase remained in Deidre's doorway. He checked her car in the employee lot. Unlocked. Her clean shirts lay across the back seat.

Back in the house, he tapped on her door again and called out louder.

Still no answer.

Liam checked the kitchen. There were two of her favorite cranberry muffins in the basket. The gym was also empty. Where else would she be? The lights in the blue parlor where they'd played games were off. Liam cleared the room anyway. She wasn't on the couch.

Liam returned to her room. This time he opened the door. Like his, the space was a two-room suite with a small sitting area and a bedroom.

"Deidre?" Liam listened at the closed bedroom door. When there was no answer, he slowly opened it. "Deidre? Are you in there? It's Liam." Scaring her was not on his to-do list. His back and head still hurt from last night's takedown.

The overhead light illuminated the room. Deidre lay on the bed, still dressed in yesterday's clothes, one shoe on. The other, still tied, lay haphazardly on the floor. Her hair lay loose around her head, framing her face in waves.

Liam debated removing the shoe, the possibility of being kicked by one of her lethal feet balanced against her comfort. "Deidre?"

"What—?" She quickly sat up, looking around. She pushed her hair back. "Liam, is something wrong?"

"No, I wanted to check on you. Your suitcase was propped in the door, and I didn't think you would have deliberately left it there."

Deidre stifled a yawn. "No, I came back in here for something. I must have fallen asleep."

"I'm glad you didn't leave, then."

She retrieved her shoe from the floor and wedged it on. "Thanks for waking me up. I'd better get going."

Liam touched her arm. "Have breakfast with me first. Cook made her breakfast casserole."

For a moment, he was sure Deidre would do the impossible and turn down the breakfast casserole.

"That isn't fair tempting me like that. How will I ever return to cooking for myself?" Deidre moved her suitcase and closed the door as she exited her suite.

"I probably shouldn't mention there is a muffin left."

"I'm already staying for breakfast. You don't need to keep giving me reasons."

Liam handed Deidre a plate off the stack. "I'm going to miss this."

"The food? Or not prepping it?"

"Eating breakfast with you. Having to make sure I'm fully awake to catch all the subtleties of your banter."

"Oh." Deidre filled her plate and took one of the muffins. "I'm going to miss conversation too. Fiona isn't much of a morning person."

They sat down at the small table. Liam waited until after she had her first bite of muffin. "That talk I asked for last night—are you ready for it?"

"Not really, but I don't think you're going to give me a choice."

"I am not sorry for kissing you."

Her eyes widened.

That wasn't where he meant to start.

"I've wanted to kiss you since that day in the spa when you nearly drowned me. I'm glad you won't be working for me anymore because I want to date you, explore the chemistry we've been trying to ignore, see if our relationship can move to a more personal level. I admire you." There. He'd spit it all out.

Deidre set her muffin down. There was only one small bite on the side. "Well, I want to apologize for the kiss. And for crying all over you. It wasn't professional and probably only added to your feelings about women in this business, although you've tried hard to accept me and my work. I shouldn't have done it. I won't deny you're a marvelous kisser, but I used you. I needed to feel something I haven't felt in a very long time—the chemical rush that comes from a good makeout session. It was messed up using you like that. I'm sorry. I wish you all the best." Deidre left her muffin on her plate and rushed out of the room.

Liam stood, prepared to run after her. And beg her to listen. A door slammed in the hallway and another beyond. Likely the door to the garage.

He could run after her. Beg her to stay.

Liam cleared the plates.

Why was she crying again? Breaking it off with Liam before they became a thing was the right thing to do. The only thing to do. The lie she'd told him about going back into her suite and falling asleep had been partially true. She had gone back to wait for him. To talk. Maybe to have his arms around her one more time. She was a sucker for hugs.

She'd paced back and forth, not daring to get in the shower because she didn't want to miss seeing him. The temptation he offered was security. Security? Oh, the word had too many meanings. More like a rush, a high. It had been a mistake to kiss him, to allow herself to feel a man could love her again. Had her ex ever loved her? Looking back, probably not. Liam said he admired her, but that wasn't love.

Deidre was as guilty of using Liam as her ex had been of using her. She would not become that woman. Besides, Liam wanted children, a family.

She pulled into her parking spot, happy to see Fiona's space vacant.

She only wanted a shower and sleep. Maybe when she woke up, she would have amnesia.

If only life were so simple.

Liam's pillow smelled faintly like Deidre. Impossible. She had only used it for five hours yesterday.

Liam glared at the red numbers on his alarm clock, willing them to change. 3:24 Sunday morning. He had an assignment in a few hours, when normal people were awake. The press conferences. Then he would take his vacation, paid or not. He needed to leave Chicago and get Deidre out of his mind. At least she hadn't strung him along for months before admitting she'd used him. Why didn't he feel used?

He pulled the pillow out from under his head and threw it into the closet. Maybe he could sleep if he didn't smell her shampoo anymore.

The clock refused to change numbers.

LIKE THE REST OF CHICAGO and probably a fair amount of the world, Deidre watched the Harmons' live press-conference broadcast Sunday morning. Brandon, Connor, and Davis made their appearance before the world from the hospital conference room. Abbie wore a blue dress and smiled for the camera. Dr. Song discussed how rare natural-birth triplets were and the precautions taken. She emphasized how she and the hospital always tried to adhere to the mother's birth plan regardless of status. The photo Preston had snapped of the boys holding each other showed on the screen. Preston managed to slip in a request for well-wishers to donate to a local charity to help mothers and children in need.

From the Dermot Security app, Deidre knew the hospital had been turning away gifts and flowers. Items left at the estate were being regifted to one of several local charities as soon as they arrived.

After the news conference, Deidre called Hastings scheduling. "Hi, this is Deidre. I guess I'm back. I wanted to check on when I would be scheduled next."

"The computer shows you are still under contract with Dermot. I can't schedule you for three weeks."

"The job is finished. Can't you change the computer?"

"Sorry, no. Alan also left a note saying you have five mandatory paid-vacation days, and he won't discuss a schedule with you unless you produce at least one receipt proving you've vacationed. And there is a PS, and I quote, 'Receipts from hardware or paint stores don't count.'"

"It's a conspiracy."

The scheduler laughed. "From what I hear, you earned it. Catching a rogue photographer without the principal noticing? And having been awake for two days? I'm impressed."

"I'm afraid you've heard exaggerated claims. Mrs. Hastings noticed my takedown, and I was only on duty a day and a half."

"Mrs. Hastings doesn't count. She notices everything. Abbie didn't notice, and that's all that matters."

"Abbie was busy. I don't think she would have noticed a troupe of clowns acrobating through the room." Deidre doodled on a scratch pad.

"Still, good job. And enjoy your vacation."

Deidre hung up. She would wait a couple of days before she argued with Alan over bringing her back on. In the meantime, she had those paint chips in one of the kitchen drawers.

Presidential motorcades were shorter. Liam watched their progress from the passenger seat of the rear vehicle. As they neared the estate, local patrol officers helped by blocking off normally quiet side streets. There was a reason someone had dubbed Mr. and Mrs. Harmon Chicago's prince and princess. Dozens of people held signs welcoming the babies.

The babies had safely reached the house in a rented minivan a half hour ago, along with the new parents and zero fanfare. The tinted windows of the family car in front of him hid the two pediatric nurse practitioners who would monitor the boys for a few more days.

At last, the vehicle Liam rode in entered the estate gates, his father and the estate supervisor meeting him at the parking garage.

"Well done. We are now back to our new normal. Fortunately, the boys don't have to leave for weeks. It's easier to send a doctor here." Simon turned to the supervisor. "I'll put the daily running of the estate back into your capable hands. My son and I are going to go recruit a few more women for Mrs. Harmon's detail."

"If you can steal Ms. Ross away from Hastings, I'll give up half my vacation days," said the supervisor.

"With the 'Use them or lose them' policy, you already do."

"Well, I won't miss them, then." The supervisor tapped his earpiece and turned away, starting a conversation with someone else.

Liam crossed his arms. "So, what is my next assignment?"

"You get a week's vacation too. Paid. I want you fresh when you recruit more female bodyguards. I didn't do too good of a job with our last ones, other than Mia." Simon unlocked his SUV. "It wouldn't be professional for us to steal Ms. Ross; however, she is on our payroll for a couple more weeks. If you got her input on finding some good candidates, I don't see where she'd have a conflict of interest. Also, the annual security mini Olympics is scheduled for August 12. Make sure we have a good team. With Abbie and Alex Hastings out, we may have a chance this year."

"Alex is out?"

"He is on a special assignment out of state."

"Wasn't he at the hospital yesterday?"

"Yes. I don't think he would have missed his sister's babies for anything. Our competition is different."

"I'll pull a team together."

"Too bad Deidre won't be on our payroll anymore." His father closed the door and drove away.

She wouldn't help anyway.

Liam drove home, wondering where he could spend his vacation so he wasn't thinking about Deidre. There was no way he could rock climb without wondering if he could have gotten her to try. Hawaii was out. Maybe Canada? They hadn't talked about Canada, had they?

19

PAINTING THE SOUTH WALL OF her kitchen in the color christened 'chocolate dream' by the paint manufacturer was a much better idea on paper than on the wall, proving Mondays could still be Mondays even if she had the day off. Deidre set down her roller. Maybe when the paint dried, it would look better, edible even. It would have been cheaper to buy a pint of every chocolate-based ice cream in the supermarket. She could counteract those calories with extra workouts. This mistake would need two coats of primer.

Her phone rang. It was the tone she used for Hastings. Deidre checked her hand for paint before answering. "Hello?"

"Are you home painting or out enjoying the summer in the Canadian Rockies?" asked Alan.

"My guess is you know the answer to that question."

"My sister would like to see you this afternoon. She asks that you drop by between three and four-thirty."

"Why?" Deidre cradled the phone and dipped the roller into the paint pan. She needed to finish the wall before she could leave.

"I don't know. Abbie didn't tell me that. Just asked me to make the call."

"When did she turn you into her errand boy?"

Alan laughed. "When she was three and talked me into stealing cookies for her."

The mental image fit. Deidre had done the same to her brothers, but they'd always turned it on her somehow. "I'll go before she asks you to break any laws, then."

"Thanks. And I am serious. I need at least one receipt from a vacation location not in the greater Chicago area. No hanging around the zoo parking lot looking for discarded stubs."

"I wouldn't do that."

"Really?"

"Not the zoo. Science museum, yes. Zoo, no."

"Bye, Deidre. Take a vacation."

Deidre finished the wall. It wasn't as bad as she first thought. With some white-framed photos, the color could grow on her.

After cleaning up and showering, Deidre pulled into the employee lot of the estate at three minutes past three. Three must be a theme around the place. She found Abbie in one of the sitting rooms next to a portable crib.

"Would you believe it? I got them three adorable bassinets, and they won't sleep unless they're together. I'm a little worried about what the future holds."

Deidre looked at the sleeping boys dressed in blue, green, and red. "Color coding?"

Abbie slipped off one of the tiny socks to show tiny green toenails. "Clothing and toenails. This is Davis. Preston's father is appalled I would resort to painting their toenails. However, until they develop enough for us to consistently tell them apart, I'm not risking mixing them up."

"Good idea."

"Come walk with me." Abbie nodded at a nanny Deidre hadn't noticed sitting in the corner. Abbie led the way into the library. "I wanted to thank you for everything you did the other day. And for the record, I really didn't see you take that guy out. I am not sure if I should be ashamed or not."

"You were pretty busy at the time. And I didn't want to do anything that might affect your blood pressure."

Abbie crossed the library and took the stairs to the workout room. "Sorry to make you walk with me here. I'm only supposed to take short, slow walks this week. I feel weird walking around the halls. I keep bumping into housekeepers and such. I think they've raised the bar to hospital sanitary. They're always cleaning."

Deidre set her own treadmill to a low speed.

"I will not ask you how hard the delivery was for you. But I want to thank you. I found this little cabin up north of Yellowstone. It's yours for the week. You've told me how much you want to run away from civilization and be in the mountains. Our plane can take you tomorrow morning."

"You can't do that!"

"I'm sure I can. Preston has given me an absolutely insane personal budget. Call this a thank-you gift." Abbie pulled out her phone. "Look at all the photos, then try to say no."

Deidre scrolled through the photos. Tall trees, wildflowers, and a sunrise taken from the perspective of the house. The rooms were modern and rustic at the same time. A jetted tub in the bathroom promised relaxation. "You had me at the sunrise. But it's too much."

Abbie stopped her treadmill. "I don't think so. I know you have the forced time off. And you can use the receipt from the grocery store in the town fifteen miles away to prove you went on vacation."

"Alan knows?"

"Of course. He brainstormed with me."

Deidre turned off her treadmill. "I shouldn't say yes. It's really too much. But I will thank you and take it. To be honest, I couldn't come up with a vacation idea I liked and could afford."

"Good. Be at the airport tomorrow morning at 6:00 a.m. The keys for the cabin and the rental car will be at the airport. You'll need to buy food, but everything else should be there."

"I can't believe you're doing this." Deidre hugged Abbie, a boundary they had never crossed.

Abbie laughed. "Make sure you enjoy yourself. Take a good book to read, find a mountain man to hike with, and take photos of the wildlife."

"Don't worry. I have so many eBooks."

"Download them before you go. I'm not sure whether the internet is sporadic or nonexistent at the cabin. Of course, you could always go into town. The local café might have free wi-fi, and you might meet some rugged mountain man."

"The only love interests I'll meet will be in my books." Book boyfriends were safe. You knew from the beginning that they would get a happily ever after with someone else.

When Deidre got home, she found the brown wall much more cheerful than she originally thought.

Liam needed to finish the reports before he began his vacation. He'd hoped to finish them on Monday, but Tuesday morning found him at his desk again, correcting an error his father found. Liam checked over the police report one last time. Where was Deidre's police statement? He thought back and realized she'd left the hospital without talking to them. Had he even relayed the message for her to go down to leave a report? No.

The phone buzzed. It was a call from the receptionist. "Liam."

"Mr. Harmon is here to see you."

At 7:50 in the morning? What was wrong now? "Coming."

Preston Harmon stood with another man Liam didn't recognize in the lobby. Liam extended his hand for a handshake. "Mr. Harmon, what brings you here so early?"

"I have a delivery of sorts to make. This is Mr. Webb. He's a contractor. He will be assisting me. I heard you liked our swim spa, so I am giving your firm one. Where's your gym?"

Liam tried to get his mouth or feet to move. "You've already given us a huge bonus."

"Let me pass on some wisdom I've learned from Abbie the past couple days. Don't argue with a sleep-deprived billionaire."

"Are the boys keeping you up?" With the nannies and the nurse practitioners at the house, he assumed they would sleep more.

"The boys are on the small side and have to be fed every two hours. It's harder on Abbie than on me." Preston covered a yawn. "Where's your exercise room?"

"Oh yes. This way." Liam led them to the back half of the building. Mr. Webb immediately started exploring, walking around the few guards finishing up their workouts.

Preston nodded at a bench. "Do you mind if we sit?"

Liam moved a stack of towels to the floor to give them both room.

"I had expected to find your father in. I'd wanted to surprise you. I understood you were on mandatory vacation."

For a sleep-deprived father of only four days, Mr. Harmon was more informed on trivial matters than one would expect. "He usually gets in around nine. I was finishing up some paperwork."

"Where are you going?"

"I thought I would drive north. No real plan. Do you mind if I send a text? I forgot to ask Ms. Ross to turn her statement about the photographer in to the police."

Preston leaned back against the wall. "She won't get it."

"What?"

"Deidre won't get your text. She's on an airplane to Montana."

"Oh. I didn't know."

"Abbie bullied her into a vacation yesterday—a week at a mountain cabin. Even sent her on our plane. Like I said, don't argue with a sleep-deprived billionaire." Preston checked his watch. "The flight time is about three hours. They left at six."

"Thanks."

"I'm surprised she didn't tell you. I thought you two may have been more than coworkers." Preston closed his eyes. "Maybe I read that wrong."

"I read it wrong too."

Preston sat up. "What are you going to do about that?"

"Not much I can do."

"Really? I realize you may not have been dating much the last couple years, being deployed and all, but I thought the military taught you to do all you can do—or is that be all that you can be?" Preston shook his head. "I think my brain is dying. My point is, you can't give up. Unless you proposed and she turned you down flat. You didn't propose, did you?"

"No."

"Good. It would be harder to get her back unless the proposal had been a fake ..." Preston blinked. "This is why I am not going into work today. I love the kids, but I need sleep. You should go find her."

"Montana is a big place."

"Yes, but I only own two properties there. And as of two weeks ago, Abbie owned only one. Mine are business related. Hers is this cabin with a hundred acres of woods for the boys to explore." Mr. Harmon ran a hand down his face. "I'm not sure where I was going with that."

"If Deidre went to Montana, she probably wants to be alone."

"As my mother says, wants and needs aren't the same. I don't know how much Deidre told you about her past, but I can't tell you anything. Let's just say being in a delivery room for nearly a day and a half and seeing the neonatal team scramble for even a moment was probably the hardest thing Deidre could be asked to do. If Abbie could, I think she'd give Deidre the cabin because she thinks nothing she can do will ever be enough thanks."

"I learned a little about her history after the fact."

"Are you good at Clue?"

"The game? No. Deidre won every time."

"The best I can do is to show you the plane's itinerary. The airstrip is about twenty miles from the cabin and two miles from the town. Any more, and I'll be in more trouble with a sleep-deprived billionaire. Figure everything else out on your own. But if you're wandering around the country, drive more west than north. I'm saying too much."

Mr. Webb returned, tablet in hand. "I found the perfect spot for the spa, and since we won't need to build any permanent structures or reroute the plumbing, we can install it today. You will, however, lose your old water fountain. But it doesn't look like it's used often anyway."

"The water tastes like old pipes. No one ever uses it."

Mr. Harmon stood. "Then let's get this in. Give you something to look forward to after your vacation." He yawned again. "Time for me to get back. Mr. Webb, do you have what you need from me?"

"I need Mr. Dermot to sign some papers."

Liam signed the forms and walked Preston to the front door. "Thanks for your gift. I had it on my bucket list to get one someday."

Preston tapped on his phone. "This is the flight plan my pilot filed. They should land in thirty minutes. You can text her your question then."

Liam made a note of the regional airport near Yellowstone.

THE LUXURY JET CIRCLED THE tiny airport twice, waiting for clearance. Lakes and mountains appeared in every direction out the small window. If Deidre had dreamed up a place, she couldn't have made it look this good. The pilot taxied to a small hangar where Deidre disembarked with her bag. A teen in jeans and a yellow T-shirt met her.

"Ms. Ross? Hi, I'm Kalina. My dad owns this hangar. Here's a key to the cabin and the remote for the garage door. Oh, and a map. You will definitely need a map. The GPS will try to send you on an old logging road. This is the address to Mama's Bakery and the grocery store." Kalina talked faster than anyone Deidre had ever met. "They won't let me drive a rental car, but if you want to put your things in the back of the truck, I'll drive you around to the commercial terminal." The girl grabbed the handle of Deidre's suitcase and walked off, Deidre hurrying after her.

"My dad always tells visitors to drink plenty of water. Some listen and some don't. Better drink water than have altitude sickness. Use the gas station by the grocery store. It's so much cheaper. Main street is mostly a tourist trap. The theater is good. I'm in *Seven Brides for Seven Brothers.* It plays tonight, Thursday, and Saturday of this week. The other show is *Anne of Green Gables.*

It's pretty good too. My little sister is the understudy for Anne. If you go, you need to buy the fudge, and I am not just saying that because I work there. It's a-maz-ing. Like the best thing I've ever tasted. My boyfriend tells me not to eat it because I will get fat." She stopped to heft the suitcase into the back of the truck.

"He doesn't sound like a very good boyfriend."

"He isn't. He's a summer worker. Next year I'll get someone better. I'm not dating any of the cowboys or Idaho farm boys who come here. As if..." She climbed into the cab of the truck. "When I turn eighteen, I'm out of here. I'll go to theater school in New York or maybe Hollywood. And I'll have an excellent boyfriend. You must have an excellent one, you're so pretty."

Deidre debated her answer and the unsolicited advice she wanted to give, starting with getting rid of the current boyfriend who wouldn't let her eat fudge, then not mentioning she *could* have had a wonderful boyfriend, but she wasn't ready or willing for the possibility of more pain. "I don't have a boyfriend right now."

"Don't you have any fun? Or are you on the rebound?"

"Of course I have fun. That's the one reason I'm here."

"Alone?" The teen pulled into a parking space in front of the rental-car lot.

"Usually with friends, but this week I will have fun on my own. Hiking, reading, and maybe coming to your musical if I can get a ticket." Deidre hopped out of the cab and felt around in her pocket for some cash to give Kalina a tip. A ten or a twenty. Deidre handed Kalina the ten. "Thanks for the help and all the directions."

Kalina pulled a card out of her pocket. Show this at the box office, and if they can, they'll get you a seat with the 10 percent off. I already signed the back. Saturday's show is probably sold out."

"Thank you."

The cobalt-blue mini SUV seemed out of place in the mountains. Too bright, too flashy. But it was that or a vehicle without four-wheel drive. Deidre opted for the blue. Once in the car, she turned on her phone for the GPS.

A text from Liam popped up. **Did you ever give a statement to Chicago PD? I'm pretty sure I forgot to mention it. Sorry. I think you can just call if you want.** Below the text was a photo of a business card from a Chicago PD detective.

Why hadn't she thought of the police Sunday or yesterday? She knew the drill backward and forward. Had it been sleep deprivation, or overprocessing what Liam said to her over their last breakfast, or trying not to think of him at all? She needed to reply.

I'll call ASAP.

She found the grocery store and made the call from the parking lot. The detective only asked a few routine questions, explaining that with the employee's confession, all they needed was a statement that she'd witnessed him attempting to get a photo. The detective took down her contact information. Deidre told him she was in Montana and might not have service all the time. He reassured her they probably wouldn't call.

After purchasing a few groceries, Deidre headed up the canyon road following the map Kalina had given her. The cabin was larger than it looked in the photos Abbie had shown her. A detached two-car garage sat hidden behind the largest pine tree in the world, or at least the parts of the world Deidre had visited. The key slid easily into the front door lock. After storing her food in the refrigerator, Deidre explored the cabin. The main-floor master had its own fireplace. Would it be cold enough at night at the end of June to use it or the variety of hot chocolates she'd noticed in the welcome basket? Deidre checked her weather app. No response and no bars. An old-fashioned rotary phone sat on the bedside table. She picked it up and heard the familiar hum of a dial tone. There were two rooms with multiple bunk beds. Deidre kept those doors closed. A loft above the living room looked out a gabled window and across the valley. Deidre tested the beanbag chairs. A perfect place to read. A smaller bedroom with a similar view of the valley, and a bathroom made up the rest of the upstairs. Deidre chose the upstairs room for the view.

From the living-room window, she watched a doe and her fawn as they ate. She turned to tell Liam—oh, she hadn't realized talking to him was such a habit. It had been nice to have someone to talk to about little things all the time.

Deidre shook her head. No. Been there, done that. She was better off alone.

Vlad the Impala had seen better days, mostly Liam's high school days. The odometer now read 286,917. A respectable lifetime of travel. Since his return to the States, Liam had mostly driven one of the fleet vehicles, and the white Chevy had remained parked in his father's garage.

Liam patted the dash above the steering wheel. "Okay, old guy. Let's do another road trip. Wisconsin?"

The engine started without a hiccup.

"Oh, so it's Wisconsin and beyond." He drove north out of the city and beyond the suburbs with no destination in mind. Soon he crossed the state line, looking for some indication of adventure—perhaps a billboard or an exit sign with an intriguing name. Nothing. The split for the I-90/I-94 loomed ahead. Liam almost wished his car dice would make the choice for him. A fifth wheel forced him to take the opposite exit.

Vlad ate up the miles on westbound I-90, neither driver nor car inclined to stop. Adventure awaited somewhere.

Deidre closed the eBook she'd finished and searched for the sequel on her tablet. The icon showed the book had not downloaded. Deidre checked for another book. The same icon appeared. Oh, for a good paperback. They didn't need wi-fi. Her list of errands now numbered three. Somehow she'd packed toothpaste but no toothbrush, and she needed to check on tickets for *Seven Brides for Seven Brothers.*

The trip to town seemed faster than the drive out to the cabin. She passed Mama's Bakery. Ah, a fourth errand. Check out the breakfast-muffin selection and whether they had wi-fi. Deidre saved that errand for last. At the grocery store, she added popcorn and a recent paperback to her purchases.

There was exactly one ticket left for the Thursday show in the center of a row. Likely, two families had taken either end. The woman behind the ticket counter gave her the promised discount plus a coupon for a piece of the famous fudge when Deidre mentioned Kalina had informed her it was the best in the world.

Both sides of the street were filled with tourist shops that had items ranging from Montana T-shirts to expensive Indian pottery. Finding the cobalt-blue SUV was easy in the mass of cars that had vied for the few parking spaces. Perhaps the color hadn't been a bad choice.

The bakery smelled divine and had a wi-fi logo on the window. Deidre chose a raspberry muffin made with local berries but passed on a tempting cream-cheese brownie for later. In the bottom corner of the display case, there were several gluten- and sugar-free choices. She would have to tell—No, she wouldn't tell Liam, and she wouldn't think about him anymore.

She logged in to the wi-fi using the password "pleasedontask." The password begged a question or two of its own but brought a smile to her face. As did the muffin. As her books downloaded, Deidre studied the bakery case from where she sat. There were more than enough reasons to return each morning. Plus, she needed to check her email and call Mom at least once during the week.

The only text was from Fiona. **Say hi to the mountain men for me!**

Deidre returned a smiley face. So far, almost everyone she'd seen, other than a few people at the grocery store, had *tourist* written all over them. And none of them resembled Fiona's description of a mountain man.

All of her emails were ads or newsletter notifications she could ignore. Her tablet pinged, indicating the download was complete.

On the drive up the mountain, she'd found the old logging road blocked off with a chain. If there was a mountain man, he'd be living up there. Perhaps she'd take an afternoon hike so she could tell Fiona she'd checked.

Vlad passed the "Welcome to Minnesota" sign at five miles over the speed limit.

Liam was only heading west, not going to Montana. There hadn't been anything in Wisconsin he wanted to explore. And since he'd forgotten his passport, Canada was out.

Vlad insisted they get off the freeway for gas. Liam needed a break as well. The tourist map didn't have any sites that intrigued him, so he continued west.

According to the next billboard, Mount Rushmore was in South Dakota. Having never been there, Liam calculated the distance. If he drove straight through, Vlad would get him there around 1:00 a.m. After driving eleven hours, Liam pulled into a small motel in a town matching it in size. He looked at the map in the lobby. Mount Rushmore was only three hours away. The town Preston had mentioned was about nine.

It didn't matter. He wasn't going to Montana. Tomorrow, he had a mountain to hike.

In his room, he searched for information and discovered that the hike to see the presidents was less than a mile. There were other trails in the area. Too bad his boots were at home in the closet. Some of the better hikes required more than old running shoes. Then where could he go?

He pushed the first thought away. And the second.

Not to Montana. Definitely not Montana. And no way would he go to Yellowstone. After all, he didn't have his hiking boots. There was absolutely no reason to go farther west, other than his heart was already there.

THE SUNRISE WAS WORTH EVERY penny of rent Abbie must have paid for the cabin. Unless she'd bought it. The thought hadn't occurred to Deidre before. Abbie had only said she found it, and it was much too nice for an Airbnb. No, Abbie hadn't said it was a rental. How much damage could a billionaire do on bed rest? She would ask when she got back.

Sitting on the porch with a cup of hot chocolate, wrapped in an afghan and watching as Mother Nature bested every painter that ever lived was the perfect way to start the day. Deidre wished she could paint or write. Either occupation would be well served by the location. She'd written some stories in high school, but how did someone write a novel? She loved to read romances but was sorely underqualified to write in the genre. Her happily ever after, sadly, had never come. In recent years, that had been her choice. If she hadn't been so tired or so in shock, would she have answered Liam differently? Could she have made a relationship work?

A bird flew overhead, another chasing after it. Mates or enemies? The line between the two could blur so fast. Liam could have been a good friend. Was a good friend. What if she reached out to him? They could be friends. He hadn't declared he loved her, just admired. They could be a mutual-admiration society.

But that kiss.

Or kisses, rather. Platonic wouldn't work for long. Sooner or later, probably sooner, she'd want more. It wasn't just because he was handsome or had abs to drool over. It was the little kindnesses and the talks they had. He'd even broken his no-carb diet and tried one of her muffins. After the initial bumps in their relationship, he'd proven he wasn't a chauvinist. Opening her doors made him a gentleman. He really was one of the good guys. Deidre covered her mouth as a giggle tried to escape and break the morning stillness. She thought of the way he had blushed when he explained he wasn't trying to make a move on her by offering his apartment. Maybe that was why he made her feel cherished. He hadn't taken advantage of her.

Not like she had of him. Not that she'd realized it when sitting in her car kissing him. Only later, when she understood the healing effect his attention had, did she comprehend what she must have done. And she was plotting to do it again—to be near him because it felt better than being alone.

A relationship with Liam wouldn't work for long. He was ready to settle down with a wife, a family, a picket fence, and a mortgage. Too bad the idea wasn't reality. Life got messy, dinners burned, schedules conflicted, and occasionally things spun terribly out of control. Could he handle it then? Or would he jump to conclusions like he had when they first met? Sometimes it wasn't anyone's fault. There was no one to blame. Life just happened.

The colors changed from pinks to yellows, then faded into blues as the sun rose above the eastern wall of the valley.

It was better that she had told Liam no. Even if for one moment she'd allowed herself to dream the same dreams he had as he'd kissed her pain away.

Mount Rushmore was more crowded than he expected. Next to him, an older couple complained about how it had been worse at Yellowstone—more cars than animals and half the people having no respect for nature. Their complaints made him want to see it for himself. According to the map on his phone, only a small part of Yellowstone was in Montana. He could go visit the Wyoming part. If he drove through part of Montana... Who was he kidding? Even Vlad wouldn't buy the tale he was spinning. He'd goofed up. Not in falling for Deidre. Or kissing her. He'd blown the timing. The more he thought about it, the more he was sure. Would now be a better time? Was a week enough distance? She would always grieve the loss of her daughter, but she didn't need to do it alone.

Four boys ran past him, their mother yelling at them to slow down as the presidents would not leave before they got there. Liam followed the trail back to the visitors' center. A group of teens argued whether or not the mountain had a back side. Liam bit his cheek to keep from laughing. Technically, the one was right. The mountain did have a back side, but if the teens expected to find carvings there, they would be disappointed.

Liam returned to Vlad and set his GPS for the little airport Preston had shown him. Once there, he could find a Realtor. There couldn't be that many cabins sold in the last month.

Vlad made a valiant effort to handle the twists and turns of the old highway, but by the time Liam reached the junction with I-90, he knew Vlad wasn't going to make the entire trip—an assumption validated by a mechanic at a truck stop outside one of the many small Wyoming towns. Parts could be ordered, but they wouldn't arrive for two or three days and would cost more than the old car was worth. If he could get a ride to the next big town, he might be able to go buy something used or rent a car. The mechanic gave him the number of a company that would buy Vlad for parts.

Liam ran his hand over the hood of the Impala. So many adventures. His first ticket. His first kiss. An impromptu drive to Florida the summer after his senior year. A flat tire the night of prom and music played too loud. Liam dialed the number on the card. And hung up before anyone answered. Then logic told him that adding new parts would only put Vlad on life-support. Liam dialed again. He imagined it was as hard as calling a mortuary after a friend passed. Now, to find a way to go another 450 miles west.

The cream-cheese-and-blackberry pastry might be the best thing Deidre had tasted in her life. She texted Fiona. **I'm in love.**

—With a mountain man?

No. A pastry. Good thing they don't need bodyguards here. I'd stay.

—For sugar, flour, and lard? Fiona's text reminded her of other conversations the past month.

You sound like—never mind.

—Liam?

I think I goofed when I blew him off.

—What are you going to do about it?

Right now, nothing. I checked the Dermot app. He is on vacation too.

—When you get back?

I thought of bringing him back some gluten- and sugar-free things they make as a peace offering.

—That's a crime.

Bringing him back food? It isn't an international flight. No food laws.

—No. Gluten- and sugar-free pastries.

They don't exactly look like pastries.

—You should text him.

I can't. I only have the app, and everyone will see.

—That could qualify for a grand gesture.

Or losing all credibility in the field. I told you about the woman who chased Alex.

—Yes.

Dermot hired her, and she chased Liam.

—Okay. App is a bad idea. But you will do something, won't you?

Probably.

—???!!!!

I'm still deciding.

—He isn't like your ex. Corrie has been telling me everything about Liam. He really is one of the good guys.

Which is why she doesn't date him?

—They kissed once in high school. She said it was like kissing her brother.

Kissing Liam had been as far from kissing one of her brothers as she could imagine. If she had kissed Liam before she'd kissed her ex, they never would have gotten married. Deidre pushed the image out of her mind with another bite of the pastry. **That makes sense, then.**

—She says he hasn't dated since his last girlfriend dumped him.

No stories. I want him to tell me.

—Like you told him about your past.

I kind of told him. More like threw up all the gritty details in one breath.

—You could write him a letter.

I don't have his email.

—No, a real letter. Those handwritten, heartfelt things.

It wouldn't get to him any faster.

—Deliver it when you get back. Or have it delivered? Either way, it will give you time to say things. I know how hard they are for you. You have never told a guy the entire story, have you?

Deidre had never told anyone the full story. Liam knew as much or more than her own brothers. **No.**

—See, write a letter.

Hmm. Maybe. I got to go. The woman behind the counter keeps looking at me, and I am done with my food. It was the best excuse she could come up with. Any more of this conversation and Fiona would give her more ideas than she was ready for.

Deidre stopped at the counter on the way out and purchased a raspberry muffin for later. Maybe the calories wouldn't count if she hiked a few miles. "I love your food. If I lived here, I would be in so much trouble."

"I'm glad you like it. Did you buy the cute cabin up past the logging road?"

"No, my vacation is a gift from a friend." So Abbie must have purchased the cabin. Hopefully with the intent of using it for her new family. The boys would love climbing all over the mountain. *Yikes. What a security nightmare that would be.*

"Oh, I thought you might be the new owner."

"I wish."

The clerk handed Deidre's credit card back. "Have a great day."

Many of the shops along Main Street were opening for the day. Since most of the other tourists weren't crowding them yet, Deidre decided now was a great time to take a peek. In the second, she found moose stationery. The "I Moose You" package seemed lighthearted enough to write Liam. *If* she chose to do that, she wouldn't have to drive back down later.

The truck driver who'd offered Liam a ride to Bozeman weighed in on several vehicles, mostly based on his experience hauling cars to dealerships. Liam used his phone to search dealerships in Bozeman for a used car that could handle driving to wherever the cabin was and back to Chicago. He'd calculated that renting a car, including miles, would cost around $1,000. A cheap used car would only set him back a bit more and give him time to make an informed decision about a new vehicle.

Liam searched website after website. Most of the used cars were more than what he wanted to pay. There was an old blue truck at least ten years older than he was. Liam doubted it would make the trip all the way to Chicago. "How would you find a used car?"

"I bought my wife a nice little used Toyota off Facebook."

"People sell cars on Facebook?"

"All the time. Let me guess—you don't spend much time on social media."

Liam scrolled to the Facebook app. "I don't think I've even opened my app this past month. I've gotten a couple of notifications, but I ignored them."

The driver applied his brakes. "That's one way to get yourself killed. Pull too close in front of a truck driver. That little red car has miles and miles of road, and he cuts me off like he's in rush-hour traffic on the Mass Pike. There's so many fool drivers on the road it's a miracle I haven't been in an accident yet. And I'll be the one who gets sued."

"It sounds like you're one lucky guy."

"Luck has nothing to do with it. My wife and my sons pray for me every day. I make sure I spend some time with the Good Book too."

"Prayer is usually a good plan. I wouldn't say it let me down this time, but I'm sure not where I expected to be." If Vlad hadn't died, he would be at the little airport by now.

"Few of us are ever where we expect to be. The question is, are we where God needs us to be?" The driver returned his truck to cruising speed.

Was this where he needed to be, or was it happenstance? "That part is hard to figure out too."

"So do you know where you're going?" The driver's question could be taken in several ways.

"In general? I have a good idea. At this moment specifically? My plan is a little more vague."

"So why are you going there?"

Liam turned his answers over in his mind before talking. "There's this woman. We worked together, and I can't get her out of my mind. Our boss paid for her to have a vacation out here for a week. I wasn't really intending to come out here at first and see her. But it feels like something I need to do. I left things undone, and I need a chance to finish them."

"Don't you mean start them?"

"Yep." They fell into silence. Liam searched for a used vehicle. He inquired about two before he got bored and started surfing. He searched for Deidre and learned her maiden name was Vuki. He wasn't sure how to pronounce it. He scrolled through the three or four photos he could see without friending her. Just as well. It felt slightly voyeuristic. He went back to searching for a vehicle. An old touring motorcycle with cargo bins was well below his price range. He messaged the seller.

Is this still available?

—Yes.

Is it in good enough condition to make it to Yellowstone and then Chicago?

—It had a tune-up. I put new tires on it last year. I can't make any promises.

Can I see it tonight?

—Depends on the time.

I should get into town about 9 p.m.

—Too late. I'll only show it before sunset. 9:17.

Very precise. **May I see it in the morning?**

—Sure, anytime after 8.

Thanks.

Liam sighed. When he told Vlad he wanted an adventure, he hadn't been so literal.

They reached Bozeman at half past eight. Liam thanked the driver and went into the truck stop. He brought up the messages he'd traded over the motorcycle. **Arrived in Bozeman. Is it too late to see the bike?**

—Where are you?

A truck stop on the east side of town.

—How will you get here?

Uber or Lyft? He had yet to check his apps to see if either worked here.

—Is there a big metal cowboy hat on top of the building?

Yes.

—I'll be there in five minutes. We'll talk.

Thanks

Liam used his five minutes to check in with his father and inform him of the demise of Vlad. It was an excuse to hear a familiar voice. Customers came and went. Liam wondered how he would know the man selling the motorcycle and would he bring it.

A tall man in a plaid shirt stopped at the end of the bench Liam sat on. "Are you the one who wants to buy my motorcycle?"

Something about the man's tone made Liam want to salute. He stood instead. "Yes, sir. Liam Dermot." They shook hands.

"Mitch Rodgers. How long have you been out, son?"

"I was discharged in March."

"Honorable?"

"Yes, sir."

"Where are you staying tonight?"

"In the closest hotel." Liam refrained from saying *sir*.

"No, you're not. I'll find you a spot in the bunkhouse. I was heading out to the ranch when you messaged me. Believe me, you won't get an Uber out there."

Country hospitality or psycho? Liam sized up the man and took the risk. "Thank you for the offer. You sure I'm not putting you out?"

"Not at all."

Liam picked up his duffel and followed the stranger out of the truck stop.

Dear Liam,

Deidre started the letter again for the eighth time.

I am running out of paper, so I have vowed I'll finish this time. I think I've finally figured out what I want to say. I know this is cliché, but it isn't you, it's me. It would be so wonderful to get to know you better, figure out if our relationship could be more, but you want to talk about the things I blurted out in the car.

I can't talk about them. Well, maybe parts, but if I do, I know I'll turn into a big, blubbering mess. Which will probably make you think I'm—never mind. Thinking about Julia is about the only time I cry. That was her name. I know you probably don't believe it, but I am not a big crier.

A tear dropped on the page. Deidre wiped it away. She was finishing this letter no matter what. Liam probably wouldn't read it, but just once, she would get everything on paper.

I won't bore you with the history we already talked about. Six months after I joined the Chicago PD, I met Thayne Ross. We flirted, then dated clandestinely. A job opened in one of the suburbs. He convinced me to apply, pointing out that if things kept progressing, it would be better. I applied because we kept dancing around the topic of marriage. At least I thought we were. We started looking at condos and things. I didn't get the job. We kept dating. Thayne pushed for us to take our relationship to another level and move in together. I wasn't willing to do either without a signed marriage certificate. My grandma said a woman who moves in with a man without being married is giving him a warm bed and clean dishes for free. She said a bunch of other things that kept me out of trouble.

Anyway... another job in one of the nicer burbs opened, and this time I got it. One of the condos we liked was closer to it. Thayne tried to talk me into buying it with him... We got married two weeks later. He wanted me to keep my maiden name, saying Vuki was so unusual. Too unusual, so I changed it to Ross. That was the first time I saw him get angry. He didn't hit me, just didn't talk to me for days. The whole silent-treatment thing. A month after we made up, I discovered I was pregnant. Thayne was ecstatic. I was nauseated.

Fast-forward seven months. I was on desk duty, and he was working longer and longer hours. He even picked up a few night shifts. He told me we could use the extra money when the baby came. One afternoon driving home from work, I was rear-ended. Just a fender bender, but it set things in motion that shouldn't start at thirty-two weeks.

From the hospital, I called Chicago PD dispatch. They said Thayne wasn't on duty. By then I was having contractions, and so I begged for them to just find him. They transferred me to his sergeant. We had a disjointed conversation about me being Thayne's wife. I assumed the conversation was bizarre because I was feeling light-headed, not because his sergeant didn't know he'd married me.

The doctors decided it was better I deliver the baby. To be honest, this part is foggy. Whether I've blocked it out or it was from the fact I was bleeding internally and no one realized it yet, I don't know. Thayne arrived before the final push that brought Julia into the world. She was whisked away. The only thing I remember is seeing a bluish baby too small to be real.

Deidre stopped and took several deep breaths. She would do this. Just this once. If she got up from the table, she would never come back.

A nurse realized I was in trouble. And everything happened so fast. They put one of those horrible-smelling oxygen masks over my mouth and nose, and I don't remember anything more.

Two days later, I woke up in ICU. My mother and grandmother were there. I asked about Thayne. They didn't answer me. I asked about Julia, and they cried with me.

Thayne eventually came to the hospital, but something was wrong. I thought he was mad because I lost the baby. We went home, and he kept working long hours. The condo felt empty, like the room we set aside for Julia. I only had a few things for her as my baby shower wasn't scheduled for another week. I returned or donated everything but the softest of pink blankets. I kept it. So you know, I pull it out every March 8. That was her birthday. If you still want a relationship, you might want to avoid me then.

The Friday before Memorial Day, Thayne came home with a female officer I'd met briefly. She was expecting, and he wanted a quick divorce so they could get married. He said since the doctors weren't sure I could successfully carry another child, he wanted to move on. (They gave me a 70 percent chance everything would be fine if I tried again. Full disclosure: I am terrified of losing another child. If we do date and marry, I know this will need to be discussed. But NOT until then.)

I gave him the divorce, and he gave me the condo. Or at least his half of it, all paid for. I kept the name Ross because it was easier to use than Vuki. And to spite him. It turns out the real reason he didn't want me to change my name was he didn't want people to realize we were married so he could carry on his affairs. Thayne was dismissed from the force shortly after our divorce. His new wife blamed me.

One day I met Alan Hastings at an event Hastings Security was working. I was impressed with the way they worked. Abbie was there, and that was the first time I thought of leaving the force. Six months later, after trying to balance the pros and cons of my career and making a sexual-harassment complaint to PR, I turned in my resignation.

When we first met, I thought you were just another chauvinistic jerk. Thanks for proving me wrong.

Even if we never get together, I will always appreciate getting to know the real you.

I feel like I should say something more, ask you on a date or something, but I don't know what to do. Call me?

Yours,

Deidre

Before she could change her mind, she put the letter in an envelope and wrote Liam's name on it, along with the address she found on the web for Dermot Security. The post office had closed over two hours ago. Deidre pulled out a blank envelope—the only paper she had left.

I will not go to Mama's Bakery until after I've posted the letter to Liam.

For good measure, she signed the note to herself as a pledge and then filled the large jetted tub so she could soak the stress away.

A rooster's crowing woke Liam. It was still dark out. The rooster crowed again. He checked his phone. Nope, nowhere near morning, even on a farm. Someone needed to teach that rooster the difference between night and day. Liam rolled over and went back to sleep.

The next noise he heard was his phone's alarm clock.

He dressed quickly. Last night, Mitch had shown him to a bunkhouse made up of small but private rooms. Nothing like in the westerns Liam watched as a kid. The conversation had been sparse, mostly involving Liam's service record and his plans for the bike. Mitch hadn't commented much, only indicated that breakfast was served at the house at seven and he should be on time.

Liam left his duffel in the corner of the porch and knocked on the door.

Mitch let him in. Two framed photos on the mantel told Liam the story that hadn't been disclosed last night. Mitch had served his country, as had his son, and Mitch was now a Gold Star father. Not an honor any family sought.

"My condolences, sir."

Mitch nodded once. "Come into the kitchen and let's talk about the motorcycle over breakfast."

Pancakes, bacon, and eggs. Despite his usual diet, Liam didn't feel right skipping the pancakes.

They ate in silence. Mitch finished first. "The bike was my son's. Last year, I put new tires on it and gave it a full tune-up. He was coming home in three weeks. Instead, he came home two weeks early. IED. He had big plans for the bike. He was going to ride to California. I suppose Chicago is just as far." Mitch handed Liam the signed title and keys. "Promise me two things. You'll find your girl and show the bike an adventure."

Liam swallowed a lump in this throat that had nothing to do with his food. "Yes, sir."

"Then she is yours."

"How much—"

Mitch held up his hand. "The bike is yours, son. You are the right person to own her." He stood and went out the back door, and Liam hurried to follow. "There is a helmet and some protective gear that should be your size. May be a bit warm in the summer, but better than road burn anytime of year. My son bought this bag to carry extra things in. From the looks of your duffel, you might need it." Mitch opened a garage door. The bike gleamed.

Liam extended his hand. "Thank you so much, sir. I'll take good care of her."

"You're welcome."

"One question. What was your son's name? I want to remember him."

"His mama named him for the same actor I bet yours did. Liam Neeson." Mitch walked toward his house without looking back.

Liam stowed his gear, looking forward.

DEIDRE READ THE NOTE SHE'D written last night. The thought of ripping up the letter on its ridiculous stationary hurt more than going into town and mailing it, so she walked out to the garage.

What if Liam didn't respond? What if the letter got lost, like the letters she'd read about in all those novels, and she spent the rest of her life never knowing, and then when she was seventy, someone found it and gave it to Liam? And what if he came and found her and he was with his son but his wife died a year ago and then she and Liam tried to build a life together in their old age?

She shouldn't have stayed awake until two in the morning reading her last eBook. Even so, it was better to deliver the letter in person to be sure he got it. Deidre put the letter in the inside pocket of her suitcase. She wrote herself another note.

I will not go buy any cranberry muffins in Chicago until I deliver this.

Then she went to the bakery.

The airstrip was actually a little airport with a domestic terminal—larger than Liam expected from Mr. Harmon's description. He followed the signs to general aviation. Someone might know the address of the cabin. A middle-aged man in blue coveralls and a teenage girl worked on an airplane.

"Hello, I'm Liam Dermot of Dermot Security. I work for the Harmon Corporation." Liam handed the man his card. "Tuesday morning, one of the Harmon planes landed here. A Ms. Ross was dropped off and is staying for a week. I am trying to contact her, but she is not answering my calls."

The man eyed him suspiciously. Technically, none of that was a lie. He hadn't tried calling, so she couldn't answer.

The teen spoke up. "I don't think she gets good service at the cabin, so she probably can't answer your calls. Why do you need to reach her if she's on vacation?"

Liam shifted his weight. "It is a personal matter."

"Can't be too personal. She told me she doesn't have a boyfriend. Told me I should dump mine because he told me I was fat all the time. I wasn't going to because then I wouldn't—"

"Kalina." The man gave her a warning look. "Sorry about my daughter. Talking comes easy to her." He handed back the business card. "I'm afraid I can't help you. That card looks legitimate and all, but if you were looking for her officially, you would know the address of the cabin. Can't be too careful nowadays. If you want any other information, you can get it from the Harmons."

Liam turned to leave. A poster for a local production of *Seven Brides for Seven Brothers* hung on the wall. He looked back at the teen, then closer at the poster.

"Yup, that's me," said the girl. "We have a performance tonight if you want to see it. But it might be sold out." She handed him a card. "That's good for 10 percent off since I signed it on the back. It really is a good show."

"Thanks, and have a good day."

Liam drove to the town. A good portion of the main street consisted of souvenir shops. With a speed limit of twenty miles per hour, Liam was able to search the windows for the wi-fi symbol. After four blocks, he moved south one street and doubled back. In the window of Mama's Bakery, a blue sign showed the wi-fi icon. It would be a bakery. Chances were they wouldn't have any keto-friendly foods. Liam parked his bike and went in anyway. Not one but three gluten- and sugar-free options sat in the lower corner of the display case, including a crustless quiche, which he ordered. Near the door there were three stands of free newspapers, one exclusively for real estate. Liam perused it while eating. There had to be a way to find recently sold properties in the area. Something Mrs. Harmon would have purchased. Maybe a Realtor could help. They probably couldn't disclose who bought the property, but properties recently sold in the area might help.

Or he could ask Mrs. Harmon.

Who would warn Deidre.

Searching for the cabin was a bad idea.

Probably the worst idea he'd had since marrying Cindy Conner on the playground in first grade and basically becoming her slave for the rest of the year.

Even if he found the cabin, he probably couldn't get within one hundred yards of it. There were sure to be security gates or something.

This had seemed like a much better idea two days ago. Liam checked his emails and messages. Nothing of interest.

Too bad he could only text or call Deidre through the Dermot Security app. Nothing like letting dispatch know he was looking for her.

To contact Mrs. Harmon, he would have to do the same thing. Unless he called Alan, and that wasn't happening.

He could wait a week. They'd both be back in Chicago, and he could find her then. Motorcycling through Yellowstone would be an adventure.

Liam rose to leave. A sign declaring that the muffins were made with local raspberries all but yelled, 'Deidre would love these.' Had she found this bakery?

If he found the cabin, he would tell her about the muffins. Liam checked the address for the local real-estate firm. It wouldn't hurt to ask.

Deidre sat in the SUV outside of the bakery texting Fiona.
I wrote the letter.

—Did you send it?

I'm worried it might get lost.

—Where is it?

In the pocket of my suitcase.

—It had better be there when you get back.

It will be.

—What are you doing today?

Eating an amazing pastry and going to 7 Brides for 7 Brothers tonight. I think I'll go hike the old logging road too.

—Maybe you'll meet a mountain man.

Ha ha. I don't think that will happen.

Two stalls over, a motorcycle roared to life. Deidre glanced at the noisy machine, prepared to find an entire gang. Only one rider, a man in a blue helmet with the visor pulled down, backed his machine up. That would be a fun way to see the mountains. The ping of another text brought her back to her phone.

—You don't dream big enough.

You dream too much. If you asked, do you think Corrie would give you his number?

—Liam's?

Yes. Who else had they been talking about?

—Maybe. She might want his permission first. Why don't you have it?

We made all our work calls through the security app. Like I do with Hastings.

—I'll ask. I gotta go.

TTFN!

Deidre was the only customer. She gave up on playing eeny meeny miny moe and purchased three different items. "Slow day?" she asked the woman behind the counter.

"No, about average. Things slow down about this time for an hour before we get the post-lunch crowd. Too bad you weren't here fifteen minutes ago. You missed a tall drink of water who ordered the crustless quiche. If keto would do for me what it's done for him, I'd be on the diet right now."

Deidre took her bags. She must be referring to the motorcyclist. "That good?"

"Yup, and he was taller than you. Not from around here, but he didn't exactly look like a tourist either."

"Too bad I missed him." Deidre took her usual table and used the wi-fi to download another book. Even if she had seen the rider without his helmet on, it wouldn't make a difference. Mountain man or not, she wanted to see if Liam was still open to dating her first.

The day had been rather unproductive. As he'd suspected, the Reltors were not going to discuss past sales—although two of them mentioned a cabin on one hundred acres that had recently sold. But they only gave vague directions such as "west" or "up the mountain," which he could have already guessed. He found a hotel with a vacancy five miles east of town. It was the sort of establishment that thrived on tourists who hadn't planned ahead. Premium prices for a lumpy bed and a questionably clean bathroom. He had slept in worse places. The chances of waking up to find that sand had worked its way into every corner of his clothing were less in this hotel than in Afghanistan. He ate dinner at a rustic-style diner that must have catered to large families. The food was reasonably priced and pedestrian.

Walking back to his motorcycle, he passed the little theater. As the teen had predicted, the show was sold out, but he could come back fifteen minutes before showtime and see if there were any cancellations. Liam thanked the kid behind the window and walked on. If he wanted to see the musical, he would stream it. The theater looked as if it had been there since the days of Kit Carson, and Liam suspected the seats would feel like they had been there even longer.

Crowds of tourists meandered down the crosswalk. Liam dodged a stroller and ended up in a western-wear shop that was much less crowded than the sidewalk. He browsed through the store thinking it would be fun to have something from Montana. A cowboy hat wouldn't work on the motorcycle, so that was out. So were the Montana-sized belt buckles, some of which could have challenged their proverbial Texas counterparts. A bandana would be useful to fill the gap between his jacket collar and his helmet—a thin bit of skin he'd never considered until this morning when a gnat or something found the spot at fifty-five miles per hour. He chose a blue one. Near the back he found a sales rack half full of long-sleeved plaid shirts like Mitch wore. Liam held a couple up. He most likely wouldn't wear one back home, but with a predicted low of forty overnight, it might come in handy here. Again, he chose blue. May as well have them match. Nothing else stood out, so he made his purchases. According to the cuckoo clock on the wall, the musical started in ten minutes.

He debated about checking with the box office until he stepped out of the store and saw a line of about a dozen people. He turned the other direction and headed to where he'd parked his motorcycle. He passed the same cobalt-blue SUV he had seen that morning. The color seemed somewhat out of place, although the license plates placed the vehicle as local. It was dirty enough to be local. The layer of dust over the back window begged for his ten-year-old self to scrawl "Wash me" across it.

Liam stored his purchases in one of the bins and drove out of town.

Cute and surprisingly professional summed up the small-town production of *Seven Brides for Seven Brothers.* Deidre stayed after to congratulate Kalina and thank her for the discount. Most of the cast stood out in the tiny lobby, shaking hands. After a brief search, she found the talkative teen selling fudge. Deidre handed her the coupon she hadn't used during intermission.

"Which kind is the best?"

"I like the peanut-butter swirl the best, but almost everyone else prefers the walnut. We used to sell white chocolate, but hardly anyone ate it."

"I'll take the peanut butter, then. You sang very well tonight. It looked like you had fun."

"It was a blast. Could you tell Gideon and I weren't getting along? He told me I was going to get fat again, and I dumped him. You were right. I should be more careful who I date. My mom is always telling me that. But she hasn't dated in for-ev-er."

Someone stood in line behind Deidre. "I better let you get to your next customer."

Deidre was two steps away when Kalina shouted, "Hey, pretty, tall lady! Did he find you?"

She turned to see if Kalina had spoken to her. "Me?"

"Ya, you. There was this handsome man looking for you this morning, but Pop didn't tell him anything." Kalina made the sale and turned to another customer. Deidre found a space against the wall and waited for Kalina to sell out. Deidre nibbled on her fudge. Kalina was right about it being the best. Deidre got back in line. When it was her turn, there were only three bags left.

Pulling out a ten, she purchased all of them. "So, who was looking for me?"

"I don't know his name. He was on a motorcycle and said he worked for the owner of the plane you came in on. Like I said, Pops wouldn't tell him a thing. If he really worked for the owner of the plane, he wouldn't have needed to ask where the cabin was, would he? We didn't think so. You look like you probably know some self-defense."

"I know a little."

"But us women have to stick together, so I thought I should warn you someone was looking for you, in case he was a stalker or anything."

"What did he look like?"

"Tall, with blue eyes like your rental car but more intense. His hair was super short, like the guys in the ROTC. He had on a motorcycle jacket, which is smart because a crash on one of those things can ruin your arms. My friend—oh, back to the guy. You could tell he was totally ripped under his jacket. Muscles like a model. I kind of believed him when he said he was a security guard. He looked like he could be. But why would a guy who isn't your boyfriend come looking for you? I asked him, and he answered in this super-deep voice. 'It is a personal matter.'" Kalina mimicked a man's voice. "I mean, who talks like that? Most guys would say 'It's personal' or 'None of your business.' He didn't even use contractions. Like it was all business that it was a personal matter. Do you know anyone with a motorcycle?"

"Not that I know of, but lots of the men I work with talk about their cars." The lobby emptied, and most of the actors had left their posts.

"Most guys around here are always talking about their trucks."

A middle-aged man came up behind Kalina and tapped her on the shoulder. "Are you talking this lady's ear off?"

"No, Pops. This is the lady that guy was looking for this morning. I was just telling her about him."

Deidre extended her hand. "Nice to meet you."

The man shook her hand. "Gordon Carrington."

"You wouldn't remember his name, would you? Kalina remembered a lot of details but not his name."

"The man handed me his card." Gordon paused, looking up and to the left. "Dermot Security. Liam Dermot. Do you know him?"

Liam was here, on a motorcycle. She'd been just feet from him. "Yes."

"If he comes around, can I tell him how to find you?"

"Yes."

"See, Pop? I told you we should have told him. He looked real honest."

Deidre turned to Kalina. "I'm glad your father waited to get my permission before giving out my information. I might not have wanted to see him."

"Really?"

"That is true. But if you see Liam, you can even tell him I drive the cobalt-blue SUV. It might make it easier for him to find me."

"You said you didn't have a boyfriend. Are you sure you want me to tell him where to find you?" Kalina's eyes sparkled with excitement.

"I never said I didn't want one."

LIAM RUBBED HIS EYES. IT was silent. What had woken him up? The phone on the nightstand vibrated with an incoming notification. He unlocked the phone to find three text messages from Corrie. He hadn't heard from her since they'd spoken after the disastrous musical last month.

11:40 p.m.

—My friend Fiona asked me for your phone number for her roommate. Should I give it to her?

11:45 p.m.

—I'm thinking not, because you said that was such a disaster. Worse than a blind date. But maybe she wants to apologize.

6:09 a.m.

—Are you even in the country or where you can get my texts?

Deidre wanted his number. That made things so much easier. He doubted she would ask for his number if she wanted to tell him off.

He responded. **I wasn't ignoring you. I was sleeping, like most normal people on vacation. Yes, give her the number.**

—Are you sure? I mean, you are on vacation and all.

Yes. I am sure.

—Okay. Are you having a good vacation?

It has been an adventure. Vlad died.

—NO!!!!!! Not Vlad. I'll miss him. How are you getting around?

I got a motorcycle. And he said he'd never need the motorcycle license he got two years ago on a bet with one of his buddies.

—Seriously? You are living on the edge, aren't you? First you get a bike, and then you let me give your number out. Should I be worried?

No. What have you been doing?

—I may have gone on a fourth date with the doctor I met at the insta-clinic.

Fourth? Will I get a save-the-date card soon?

—Stop it. I've gone on a fourth date before. I could ask you the same thing. When was the last time you gave your number out?

No comment. Have a good day.

—Bye. Be nice when she calls!!

Liam reread the conversation. How long would it take before Deidre got his number? Corrie would probably have sent it in a separate text screen even as they were typing, but the teenager at the hangar yesterday said there might not be cell service at the cabin, so it could be hours. He searched for something to stream to pass the time.

The sunrise wasn't as calming as it had been the last two mornings. Deidre bounced her foot as if the movement would hurry the sun over the horizon. She needed a good run. Fiona hadn't texted back last night before Deidre left town. And there was no point of waiting at the bakery until Fiona took her break for a text about a number she must not have gotten.

The sun touched the valley floor, chasing the shadows away. Somewhere out there was Liam on a motorcycle looking for her. Well, he probably wasn't on his motorcycle right now. She would hear it echoing throughout the silent valley. If only she'd looked up from her texting yesterday. Like one of those videos trying to convince teens they were letting the world go by while they stared at their phones. It had really happened.

She might have screamed if she'd seen him. She hadn't been ready to see him yet. The letter. She needed the letter. If he asked, she would hand him the letter and let him read it. It would be so awkward sitting there while he did, though. Maybe she should give him the letter and ask him to come back after he'd read it.

"Liam." She sent the name out to the sunrise, testing it on her tongue. The word caught in the air and hung there, creating a shadow of its own, waiting for the sun to touch it too. The letter it would have to be. Finally, the sun rose high enough to illuminate the entire valley.

Deidre couldn't wait anymore. There was a raspberry muffin calling her name, and maybe Fiona had a phone number. She checked her reflection in the mirror one last time, and then again. He'd gone to the bakery yesterday. Maybe he would come back for breakfast today. Deidre ran for the garage and the cobalt-blue SUV.

Liam sighed as the closing credits to the eighties sitcom ran across the screen. He checked the time. Past nine? He must have fallen asleep. The hotel lobby's continental breakfast was comprised of off-brand boxed cereals, cowboy-hat shaped waffles, and artificially flavored store-brand yogurt. An empty pan of what may have once been eggs sat on a warmer.

Liam headed for the bakery he'd found yesterday.

The girl from the airport was hanging a sign on the door as he entered.

"Hey, mister. I saw her last night. She came to the musical. I was right. It was sold out. We had a good night."

What if he'd gone back? Would he have seen her?

"Then Pops told her your name, and she said we could tell you how to find her." She pulled a wrinkled paper out of her pocket. "This is the address. GPS will tell you to turn on the old logging road, but it's blocked off. You can probably make it on your bike, but the better way is to go past the logging road to the next one, the graveled drive. But be careful on gravel with a motorcycle. They can spill. Also, she said I can tell you she's driving a cobalt-blue SUV."

"What color is cobalt?" There had been that bright-blue SUV in the parking lot yesterday when he'd left, and then, last night, the one he wanted to write on the window.

"It's like the blue dress on this poster. You just missed her. I passed her as I came into town. I have to hang up more posters."

That had to be Deidre. Three times! He'd been so close. If he believed in Greek gods, there would be one in big trouble right now. "Thank you for the information—Makalina, was it?"

"No, Kalina. She said you used to be her boss. Is that true?"

"Pretty much."

"But now you want to date her, don't you? And you drove all the way across the country to find her. That is so romantic. Just like a Hearthfire move. I love the Hearthfire channel. Everyone gets a happily ever after. I read online that one couple had their first kiss as extras on a Hearthfire set and now they're married. Isn't that the best? I think you should date her. I so ship you together."

"Ship?"

"Ship. You know like *relationship*. The last thing she said last night was that she would be interested in a boyfriend. I think she was talking about you. I hope she was. If it works out, you have to let me know." She held up her stack of posters. "I gotta go. I still have ten stores on my list. I am going to be so late for work out at the airport, but Pops will be glad I found you. Bye." She was out the door before Liam could respond. He had never met a person who talked so fast.

Liam ordered two of the broccoli-and-three-cheese egg cups to go. The woman behind the counter also handed him a carefully wrapped cream-cheese brownie.

"I didn't order that."

"No, but if Kalina is right, and you are looking for a tall woman with long dark hair, you will need this when you find her. Believe me, she has been looking at this brownie section every day this week. Food may be the way to a man's heart, but chocolate is the way to a woman's." She wouldn't accept money for the brownie, so Liam stuck a ten in the tip jar.

Before putting on his helmet, he studied the map, then followed the road west out of town.

SHE'D CHICKENED OUT.

Although Fiona had given her Liam's phone number, Deidre couldn't get her fingers to dial more than the area code. She rounded the last curve back to the cabin, the one where the bars for cell service disappeared. Deidre contemplated going back to town, but the road wasn't wide enough or safe enough for her to turn around. She could practice calling at the cabin and go back at lunchtime if she hadn't heard from him by then. Not that the chances of Kalina or Pop running into him were very high.

She left the SUV outside the garage to force herself to go back out later. A run was what she needed right now. Or a hike. Definitely a workout, though. But if she went too far from the cabin, she would never get in the car and go back to town. Treadmills were not something people kept in vacation cabins. Deidre opted on doing laps around the wraparound porch.

She pretended to talk on the phone. "Hi, Liam? This is Deidre ... Fiona got your number from Corrie ... I hope you don't mind ..." That was lame. She switched her phone to the other ear. "Hi, Liam, this is Deidre. I know I was pretty rude last time we talked ..." Better? Worse? She spoke to men every day of her life. Being the minority gender in her occupation, she had to. She took a deep breath. "Hey, Liam—" No, it still felt wrong. She stopped pacing and found a spot with her favorite view. "Hi, this is Deidre. I heard you were in town. I think I goofed up when I told you I didn't want to see you. I'd like to see—"

"You would?"

Deidre jumped and spun around, her cell phone flying out of her hand and over the deck's banister. Oh, gosh. Tall drink of water in jeans and a leather biker jacket. "You scared me."

"Didn't you hear me drive up?"

"I am embarrassed to say no. I was trying to figure out what to say when I called you."

He took a step closer. "It sounded like you were leaving me a voice message."

Deidre backed up until she hit the banister. Any farther and she would join the phone. "No cell service up here. I was practicing. Trying to figure out what to say."

"It sounded like a good start to me."

"It was better than some others." She needed more time. "How did you find me?"

"There is this girl Kalina. I think you know her. Talks incredibly fast. I ran into her this morning at the bakery, and she told me how to get here."

"She was walking in as I left. You must have gotten there right after me."

"I think we've been within just feet of each other a few times in the past couple days."

Deidre nodded. "Yesterday morning I was texting Fiona, asking for your phone number, when you got on your motorcycle. If I had looked up …"

"Then last night the musical was sold out. I saw the line and the blue SUV."

"That's three misses. Does that mean we're out?"

Liam continued to move closer. "I don't think we're playing baseball."

Deidre inched to the side. She could not do a kiss, not yet. "No. I have something for you. I need you to read it. If you still want to talk afterward, I'll be over there on the logging road, heading up the mountain. There's this big boulder the size of a large SUV. I'll wait there—as soon as I find my phone." She pulled the folded letter from her jean pocket where she'd put it that morning, careful not to touch his fingers as she gave it to him.

He looked from the letter to her. "You are sure this is what you want? You don't want to talk?"

Deidre closed her eyes for a moment and took a deep breath. She opened them and looked directly into his. "I do want to talk, just not about what's in that letter. I don't think I can say the things I need to … that I need you to know. Things I can't—"

"I think I understand. I'll come find you after I read it."

"Even if you don't—?" That thought was another thing she didn't want to put into words.

"I will come." Liam reached into his coat pocket. "I hope I didn't smash this too much. The baker assured me it would help me plead my case."

"How did she know you were coming here?"

"Kalina," they said in unison.

Deidre opened the bag. "Cream-cheese brownie. She chose well. I've been contemplating this one for days."

"Save me a bite?"

"Really? It isn't keto."

"I know, but I learned something from a stack of pancakes yesterday."

"What?"

"I'll tell you after I read your letter."

Deidre ran down the steps to find her phone.

The letter was smudged in a couple of places. As Liam read, he found the pages blurring from his own tears. The silly moose cartoon on the letter certainly didn't match its contents. He folded the letter and zipped it into his jacket pocket. He might read it again someday, though Deidre wouldn't see it again unless she asked. Mrs. Harmon had known at least part of what Deidre would sacrifice to guard her in the delivery room. The cabin and vacation must be an apology of sorts. He couldn't believe Deidre had accepted the job. PTSD was the name they gave it in the military. He'd survived his tours without it, but many of his buddies hadn't. No wonder she hadn't wanted to talk the next morning. What was he supposed to do with this information?

He knew what not to do. Rush her. Murder Thayne Ross, even if he wanted to. Leave her waiting too long on the old logging trail.

The day grew warm. Liam shed his leather jacket and took the steps to the yard below. Deidre's dusty footprints were easy to track. It was obvious she'd hiked this road several times. He rounded a switchback and found her sitting on a large bolder, her back to him. She turned slightly, her finger to her lips, and pointed to a meadow below where a doe and her fawn ate their lunch.

Liam crept forward using the stealthy step he'd learned in training. At the boulder, he climbed up without making a sound and slid an arm around Deidre. She leaned into his embrace. They sat in silence for several minutes before a birdcall spooked the doe and she bounded off into the trees with her fawn.

Liam adjusted his position so he could look Deidre in the eyes while still holding her. "I'd call you, but I don't have cell service."

The skin between her eyebrows crinkled. "What?"

"The last line of your letter asks me to call you."

"Oh, right. I was going to mail it, but I was worried about it getting lost."

Liam smoothed a lock of her hair out of her face. "I like your hair down."

"It isn't very practical most of the time. I keep thinking of cutting it off."

"I won't tell you not to."

"But?"

"I'd appreciate it if you would wait awhile so I can enjoy playing with it." He twisted a lock around his finger. "Unless it bothers you."

"No, you don't need to treat me like I'll break. I'm still the woman who tossed you on your back."

"I am aware of that. I want you to realize I see you as a woman, a very capable and desirable one. One I still want to date. And if those dates include workouts or sparring, that's good too. Although I would like to win occasionally."

"You won plenty of times."

"So, I'd like to ask you again. I think we make a great team. I want to explore if there's something more here and if we could eventually turn it into a permanent partnership."

Deidre turned away and reached for something. Half of the brownie sat on the paper wrapper. "Brownie?"

"Is that an answer?"

"No, it's me trying to be cautious when I don't want to be. If you are eating a brownie, I get a bit more time."

Liam took the brownie and bit off half of it, then fed the other half to Deidre. What did she need time for?

"So, what did you learn from pancakes?"

"That sometimes it isn't about what you eat as much as who you eat it with. I get philosophical on the bike. I think I knew it last week when I tried one of your muffins. I wouldn't choose to eat it if I was alone, but I wanted to share the moment with you."

"And I left."

"You know I am not him, right? But I'm not perfect either. I'm going to do stupid things."

A breeze blew a lock of hair into her face.

Liam tucked it behind her ear. "Four weeks ago, I didn't think we could trust each other enough to complete a work assignment.

To know that you trust me enough to write this letter…" He swallowed, overwhelmed by the emotions he wanted to give words to. "I love you, Deidre." He leaned in for a kiss.

She met him halfway and matched him, touch for touch, breath for breath. A hawk screeched, and they pulled back.

Deidre giggled.

Not the reaction he expected from the best kiss of his life.

Her giggle became a laugh.

Liam looked around self-consciously.

Deidre put her hand over her mouth. What was wrong with her? "I'm sorry. I just noticed your shirt."

"What is wrong with my shirt? I bought it last night."

"It's the plaid. Fiona has been teasing me about finding a mountain man like on the cover of one of the books. They all wear plaid. And we are on a mountain. And I sound just like Kalina. I'm talking too fast."

Liam knew one way to stop her, their kiss tasting of chocolate, cream cheese, and heaven.

Epilogue

Two years later

Deidre worked to calm her breathing, searching for a happy place in her mind like they'd told her to in birthing class. The cabin. Always their cabin. Technically Abbie held the deed, but in Deidre's heart, it was theirs. The place they'd spent their honeymoon early last spring, with snow still on the ground.

Another contraction pulled at her, breaking her concentration. She searched for Liam's eyes. They were filled with more love and tenderness than on their wedding day. Leap Day. He'd looked a hundred times more handsome in his wedding tux than he had on their first disastrous date, and he'd been hot then. Even now, he—

Breathe in, hold, breathe out.

The contraction passed and left her feeling like she'd completed a workout in the gym. Not that she'd had a good workout in the last five months. Hastings had put her on desk duty as soon as she started showing. Not that she blamed them. She wouldn't want to lose her baby because some rabid fan stormed the stage and they got into a fight. Even Mortimer could beat her now. She would need months to get back in shape, but it would all be worth—

Pain like nothing she'd ever felt ripped through her, and she squeezed Liam's hand to share it. "You. Are. Sleeping. On. The couch. For-ev-er!"

Liam made the stupid breathing face they'd taught him in birthing class.

The nurse-midwife said something and smiled encouragingly. Deidre pushed because her body wanted to, then pushed again.

A baby's cry reached her ears.

"It's a girl!"

As they laid the red, messy, crying baby on her chest, Liam leaned his head close to hers. "You did it."

Deidre rolled her head to the side. "No, we did. And you don't have to sleep on the couch forever. Maybe just until our anniversary."

Liam made the face that always made her laugh.

Deidre breathed in the fresh smell of her baby, and her heart softened. "How about just tonight? They have a lovely Naugahyde couch you can sleep on."

"I can live with that."

Promising to bring her right back, the nurse took the baby.

"You still like the name?" asked Liam.

"Kalina Rose." Deidre winced as the nurse-midwife kneaded her stomach. "Kui Vuki will be happy I used Rose for her great-granddaughter."

"You know, the next time we go visit the cabin, Kalina will tell everyone she got us together."

"She won't have time. She's too busy codirecting this summer's play."

The nurse came back with little Kalina all clean and bundled in a blanket.

And Liam kissed them both.

acknowledgements

My son named his first car Vlad the Impala. Unfortunately Vlad died a less than noble death when … We don't talk about Vlad's fate, but for the record my son was not in the car.

The name Kalina appears in this book as her grandmother Madelynn supported a great cause and chose a name for this book. I love your name.

As always, thanks to Tammy and Nanette who are so willing to help make all my projects better and to read for all my mistakes. I would never make it through a day without Sally and Cindy whose advice keeps me going. Thank you wonderful ladies.

Michele at Eschler Editing does the best edits; any mistakes left in this book are not her fault. Nor are my excellent proofreaders to be blamed. Thank you ladies and gents!

My family, for sharing their home with the fictional characters who often got fed better than they did. And my husband who encourages me every crazy step of the way and puts up with all my messy spreadsheets.

And to my Father in Heaven for putting these wonderful people, and any I may have forgotten to mention, in my life. I am grateful for every experience and blessing I have been granted.

LORIN GRACE WAS BORN IN Colorado and has been moving around the country ever since, living in eight states and several imaginary worlds. She graduated from Brigham Young University with a degree in Graphic Design.

Currently, she lives in northern Utah with her husband, four children, and a dog who is insanely jealous of her laptop. When not writing, Lorin enjoys creating graphics, visiting historical sites, museums, and reading.

Lorin is an active member of the League of Utah Writers and was awarded Honorable Mention in their 2016 creative writing contest short romance story category. Her debut novel, *Waking Lucy,* was awarded a 2017 Recommended Read award in the LUW Published book contest. In 2018 Mending Fences with the Billionaire, also received a Recommended Read award.

You can learn more about her, and sign up for her writers club at loringrace.com or at Facebook: LorinGraceWriter

Made in the USA
Las Vegas, NV
01 October 2021

31491731R00121